W9-AXG-092

WON'T YOU BE MY NEIGHBOR?

"Are you sure this is a good idea?"

Dacos regarded President Grig Holma with a shrug. "I want to meet these people."

"Dara?"

"Grig, it's the opportunity of a lifetime."

"Well, be careful up there, you two. Will you be armed?"

"Absolutely not," Dara replied firmly.

"Are you sure that's a good idea? I've read these people's history. They're animals."

Dacos waved his hand at the sit-map spanning an entire wall of the room. A huge formation of aircraft was moving eastward toward Lepang, while a giant naval armada was heading rapidly toward Vidare.

"Yeah, well, so are we . . ."

Ace Books by J. D. Austin

BOBBY'S GIRL
SECOND CONTACT

SECOND CONTACT

J. D. AUSTIN

ACE BOOKS, NEW YORK

If you purchased this book without a cover, you should be aware that this book is stolen property. It was reported as "unsold and destroyed" to the publisher, and neither the author nor the publisher has received any payment for this "stripped book."

This is a work of fiction. Names, characters, places, and incidents either are the product of the author's imagination or are used fictitiously, and any resemblance to actual persons, living or dead, business establishments, events, or locales is entirely coincidental.

SECOND CONTACT

An Ace Book / published by arrangement with
the author

PRINTING HISTORY
Ace mass-market edition / November 2001

All rights reserved.
Copyright © 2001 by Joshua Dann.
Cover art by Michael Koelsch.
Text design by Julie Rogers.

This book, or parts thereof, may not be reproduced in
any form without permission.
For information address: The Berkley Publishing Group,
a division of Penguin Putnam Inc.,
375 Hudson Street, New York, New York 10014.

Visit our website at
www.penguinputnam.com

Check out the ACE Science Fiction & Fantasy newsletter
and much more on the Internet at Club PPI!

ISBN: 0-441-00879-8

ACE®
Ace Books are published by The Berkley Publishing Group,
a division of Penguin Putnam Inc.,
375 Hudson Street, New York, New York 10014.
ACE and the "A" design
are trademarks belonging to Penguin Putnam Inc.

PRINTED IN THE UNITED STATES OF AMERICA

10 9 8 7 6 5 4 3 2 1

forlorn´ hope´, *obs.* a group of soldiers assigned to perform some unusually dangerous service. (1530–40; folk-etymological alter. of D *verloren hoop* lit., lost troop)

—*Random House Dictionary of the English Language*

PROLOGUE

MILLIONS of years ago, when the Earth was primarily a primordial ooze, a similar event was occurring elsewhere in the universe. Galaxies away, so far that even astronomers referred to it as simply "way the hell out there," another planet was painfully inching its cosmological way forward. This planet, which would later be called Kivlan, was thousands of years ahead of Earth in its development. That is to say, scaly crawlers were just beginning to ease themselves out of the ooze.

The planet itself began to shape up rather nicely. Polar ice caps thawed and cracked and melted and meandered their way down into wide oceans; the surface crust pushed and shoved and elbowed high mountains into existence; and broad fertile plains unfurled a blanket of plenty throughout Kivlan's temperate zones.

Amoebae gave way to creepy crawlies and amphibious reptilians, who filled out on their seafood diets and began inching painfully out of the slime, in hopes that a land-based menu would offer even more variety than their current fare.

In time, amphibians shed their scales and fins, now made redundant, and started the painful evolution into walking their planet upright. And thus socialization commenced.

Kivlan offered few caves, hence the notable absence of cavemen. Kivlanian shelter consisted mostly of animal skins worn about the body or stretched over a wood lean-to. The use of wood for construction, hit upon one day by an enterprising but ultimately forgotten Kivlanian, began relatively early in planetary history. It would later help to define the Kivlanian character; it was not that they were inherently industrious, but rather that they enjoyed comfort and ease, and would do anything to avoid discomfort. Much of the planet's development, one historian would later note, was motivated not by character but by an uncontrollable urge to lie down.

This pattern emerged as early as the origins of the mating process. At first it was as on Earth, lacking in romance and panache, consisting of a conk on the noggin of a likely female by an amorous swain. But this soon proved unworkable, as Kivlanian women were as aggressive as the men, and every bit as often it would be the male of the species who would awake the next morning sporting a large bump on the cranium. Both sides admitted that the big problem with this more violent sort of courtship was that it was simply too much work; a wink and a smile and mutual attraction proved more effective and ultimately more enduring and rewarding than a club and a fist, and it conserved energy for the more pleasurable aspects of the mating process.

The Kivlanian quest for comfort was even more evident in the history of its civilizations. Its Stone Age was shorter; its Bronze Age was longer; its Industrial Revolution came sooner. The Dark Ages couldn't be over and done with soon enough for Kivlanian tastes. A major detour on its parallel development course with Earth concerned Kivlan's revolutionary leaders. Unlike that of Earth, nowhere in Kivlan's history emerged a leader who championed austerity and self-denial. Oh, there may have been a few, but they were quickly dismissed and reduced to mere footnote status. Kivlanians were blessed with an innate sense of justice and fair play, but this was never equated with a lack of appreciation for the creature comforts.

Nevertheless, there were those nations who cast hungry eyes upon their neighbors, and leaders who thirsted for more power than was rightfully their own. Kivlan was therefore plagued with constant war and all of its attendant terrors until three hundred Earth years ago, when an international congress of scientists announced a great discovery: the harnessing of what is known on Earth as zero-point energy. This process, which converted virtually anything anywhere to cheap and efficient energy, in one sweeping gesture granted every nation its independence. Wars of expansion were suddenly and permanently rendered obsolete because every nation could now manufacture everything it could possibly need. And with this new energy source, advances came quickly and changed the face of the planet forever.

Therefore, by Earth year 2039, the planet of Kivlan was indeed a pleasant place to dwell. Its twenty-seven nations coexisted and traded peacefully, its people treated each other with courtesy and understanding, no one had to work particularly hard, and the planet itself glowed with contentment. Even its name, Kivlan, was the word for "tranquility" in an earlier, dead language.

Which made it all the more puzzling why, when the Earth ship GSS *Lifespring* entered its orbit and hailed its communications frequencies, its answer came with a shot across the *Lifespring*'s bow.

ONE

THE project coordinator of the GSS *Lifespring* was named Keith. This meant that he was in nominal command of the ship, but ever since the transfer of NASA to the stewardship of the United Nations, the military and all traces of its involvement had been expunged from the space program, except for pilots, who were of necessity hired on a contract basis. NASA was now GASA, the first letter of the acronym standing for *Global* instead of *National*, although it was still the United States who picked up most of the tab.

Keith was not, nor had he ever been, in the military. He held an impressive list of degrees in astronomy, anthropology, and astrobiology. The term "project coordinator" suited him mightily; he felt that the title *captain* or *commander* was offensive, as it implied superiority to the other members of the crew—or, rather, collective.

Keith's second-in-command—that is, his associate project coordinator—was Naomi, a former professor of environmental cosmology at the University of Oregon.

The four other mission specialists in the collective were Harry, a sociologist; Magda, a biochemist; and Jeff and Rick, two ecology activists who had been together in everything since middle school. Only Ralph, the pilot, was a military man, and he kept mostly to himself.

There actually wasn't much for Ralph to do beyond monitoring the spacecraft's control systems. Only when the craft reentered the Earth's orbit and glided into Edwards would he ever have to even touch the joystick. Ralph secretly worried that his flying skills might deteriorate after nine months in space and result in a less-than-perfect, which meant unacceptable, landing. But for now there was little else for him to do besides stay in shape on the aerobicizer and read.

The extended-range craft had been in space for almost five months, and was closing in on its target planet— although Keith refused to use the term *target* as it implied hostility and could therefore be considered offensive. He instead referred to it as the *final destination*, which Ralph thought even worse, as it implied Forest Lawn.

A crack international team of physicists, cosmologists, astronomers, and mathematicians had after years of study determined the planet nearest to Earth in distance from its sun, age, and livability. These determinations were still largely in the realm of theory when the *Lifespring* was launched from Cape Canaveral, but GASA believed it worth the risk and the UN believed it worth the USA's money.

The USA certainly didn't seem to think so, but they had little choice. America, still miffed at the fact that the UN seemed to exist only to censure it at every turn, had held back its dues for forty years. Given a choice between expulsion and underwriting space travel, they found the latter to be far less costly. While the UN Space Exploration Committee was comprised mostly of representatives from countries that had never had a space program, some former NASA chiefs were retained as consultants.

These consultants, who were in charge of crew selection, had gleefully and maliciously stacked the deck with idealistic environmental activists, who they believed would be in for a rude awakening at their first wide-eyed contact with extraterrestrials.

As it turned out, the consultants were absolutely right.

AS the *Lifespring* entered communications range with the planet Kivlan, Keith was attempting to tactfully rebuke Ralph on his choice of reading matter. Ralph, a former Navy pilot who had become a voracious reader to pass the time at sea, was idly wondering if it would take one punch or two to render Keith unconscious, given the artificial gravity in the cabin environment that was not quite as Earthlike as advertised.

"I don't understand, Keith," Ralph was saying. "How can what appears on my personal screen and goes into my head be offensive to anyone else in the crew?"

"Because it breeds a certain attitude," Keith replied. "The cr-collective should have a relationship of respect—"

"Wait a minute," Ralph interrupted. "Naomi got upset because I read Shakespeare—who she considers racist and sexist and offensive. Okay, fine. I switch to Jane Austen, arguably one of the greatest writers who ever lived—and a woman, so she can't possibly find anything sexist about that. But she does. But I'm easy. So now I'm reading Ibsen—*A Doll's House*—"

"The very title is chauvinistic," Keith said. "It implies—"

"Have you ever seen it, or read it?"

"No, but—"

"Do you know what it's about? It's about a woman who ultimately empowers herself and escapes from a suffocating lifestyle that—"

"Ralph. We all have to work together, and a little mutual respect doesn't—"

The communications console beeped. Ralph sprang into action. "We're there," he said calmly.

"Monitor all frequencies," Keith ordered, then added, "please."

Naomi entered the bridge. "Are we there?" Her eyes were shining. Keith went over to her and took her hands in his own. "Yes, Naomi. We are on the verge of a new age."

Why didn't they just hop into the sack already and get it over with, Ralph wondered. It was beginning to get a little nauseating. Oh, that's right—it would be offensive to the other members of the *collective* who weren't getting any.

"Launch the communications package," Keith told Ralph.

"Launching in three, two, one, launched." The communications package was in English, which many in the program considered offensively chauvinistic, as more people on Earth spoke Spanish, Chinese, and Hindi, but the consultants overrode these strenuous objections. The package included an English language and grammar omnibus, CDs of Mozart and Beethoven, a message of peace, a history of Earth civilization, Isaac Asimov's *Chronology of the World*, and unbeknownst to anyone, the complete works of Shakespeare, *The World's Filthiest Jokes*, and a CD of Frank Sinatra's greatest hits, downloaded by Ralph. It would take another three weeks to reach Kivlan's orbit, by which time the planet's computers, if they had them, could assimilate this new information.

"Ralph, how long before we reach the planet's orbit?"

"Uh, do you think that's a good idea, there, Keith?"

"Why wouldn't it be a good idea?"

Ralph noticed an incipient eye roll from Naomi, but decided to press on. "How do you know we'll be welcome? Just asking, there . . . Keith."

"Because the·planet is approximately the same age as our own. Virtually the same distance from its sun. Their development would have to be at least somewhat parallel—"

"What makes you automatically assume it's going to be a *kumbaya* deal? Isn't that a little bit chauvinistic in itself? How do you know they're not a bunch of morons? Or savages? Or if they are as advanced, or more advanced than we are, how do we know they don't just get off on blowing people away to pass a lazy afternoon?"

"Oh, come on!" Naomi exploded.

Ralph turned away. "Fine. Do what you want," he said tersely. He stewed for a moment and then turned back to them. "But at the first sign of trouble, I'm going to bust the gate and we're out of there. No matter what your orders are."

Naomi put her hand on Keith's shoulder. "Don't mind him," she said soothingly.

Keith took off his glasses and rubbed his eyes. "No," he replied. "Ralph does have a point. And he's only concerned for our safety. I think what we have to do now is study everything from the planet that we can at this distance. Monitor all communications frequencies if there are any, and run a tape analysis, see if our computers can make any sense of their languages, and if we can, have Harry try to make a determination of their social structure. Uh, the chemicals from their atmosphere. The weather, the—"

"Yes, *sir*," Naomi said.

"Oh," Keith gave an embarrassed chuckle, "I mean, these are just suggestions. You don't have to do any—"

"Jesus wept," Ralph sighed.

THE crew was seated at the circular conference table. Keith was glad the table was round, because anywhere he sat would not imply superiority to the other members of the collective.

"Who wants to kick it off?" Keith asked, then winced because "kick it off" was a football term, and that was an offensively chauvinistic game that celebrated violence in an allegory of fascist militarism. "I mean, who wants to go first?"

Harry, the sociologist, raised his hand. "I will, if it's okay with everyone else. Our computer has been able to distinguish forty-eight different languages so far, although they seem to fall into eight or nine groups."

"How do you mean?"

"Well, it's like our own language groups, say, Romance languages for example. To someone completely unfamiliar with our planet, French, Italian, Spanish, and Portugese would seem so much alike that it would be hard at first to tell them apart. The same would hold true for the Teutonic languages, such as German, Dutch, Danish—"

"What about the social structure?" Naomi interrupted.

"Now that's interesting," Harry said. "The stronger frequencies seem . . . guarded."

"What do you mean, guarded?"

"Communications are somewhat cryptic. I really can't make any sense out of them. Of course, the weaker frequencies, probably local stuff, while I can't make any sense of the language . . . the rhythm seems, well, in one instance, several instances, like . . . sports."

"Sports?" Keith asked.

"Yes, a kind of high-pitched excitement by one speaker followed by a crowd noise." He put his hands up to his mouth and approximated the sound of cheering from the bleachers.

"What about music?"

Magda, the biochemist, also held graduate degrees in music and music history. She was extremely bright and rather shy, but blossomed when she sang or gave a performance on her mini-piano.

"I didn't know what to expect," she said. "Having been raised on sci-fi movies, I thought music from another planet would be in a sort of New Age, electronic style. But it isn't. The first and strongest sounds I heard I could swear came from a bagpipe—a lonely, haunting melody."

"That makes sense," Naomi replied crisply. "Weren't the first instruments on our planet made from animals?"

"Well, wooden reeds, but then animals, yes," Magda said. "But the interesting thing is, there's a notable absence of brass. There are strings and reeds—or what sounds like them, anyway—but what really got my attention is that their most popular music, or at least the most predominant, has a beat. I would even say, a *back* beat."

"A back beat?" Ralph asked. "Like rock and roll?"

"Yes," she replied. "One thing I am almost certain of, these people like to dance. It's not music you can sit still and listen to. The beat is far too insistent."

"All right," Keith said, deciding to move things along. "Planet makeup. Jeff and Rick?"

It was always Jeff and Rick, never Jeff *or* Rick.

Jeff spread his hands. "Well. Nitrogen-based, maybe a tad more oxygen in the mix than ours, but definitely livable. And here's the really good part: It's a clean planet. Minimum fluorocarbons, and an ozone layer that seems wholly intact."

There was a collective sigh of relief around the table.

" 'Really good part,' you said," Keith remarked. "Is there a bad part?"

Rick looked at Jeff, who nodded. "Well, yes," Rick said. "There's another element in the atmosphere. It's new, that is, it's not part of the chemical makeup of the atmosphere. And it's only coming from a few points on the surface."

"Do you know what it is?"

Rick shook his head miserably. "I haven't a clue," he said. "It's nothing I've ever seen, and Magda—she told us she's never seen it, either."

"Hmm," Keith mused. "Ralph? You've been pretty quiet. What do you think?"

Ralph leaned back and folded his arms. "Well, I've been listening to you guys and just taking it all in. Just sort of adding it all up."

"And what's the sum of your thoughts?" Naomi asked stiffly.

"Oh, let's see what we've got so far. We've got a planet with highly active but guarded communications frequencies. A jumble of rock and roll stations, with a lone mystical bagpipe channel. We've got a clean planet with its atmosphere being suddenly polluted by the emissions of an unknown chemical at a few points on its surface. Well, it's just a theory, sports fans, but I say we stand this ship on its ear and shag ass for home."

There was an explosion of protests from around the table. "What are you *saying*?" Naomi demanded.

"I'm saying that we take what info we have and consider ourselves ahead of the game. We've done it, we've found another planet with life like ours. We've more than enough to keep our scientists busy, and we can always come back later."

"But *why*?" Keith was almost in tears.

"It's obvious to me, Keith old pal. This planet is at war."

NO one in the crew spoke a word to Ralph for the rest of the week except in the course of duty. One night, he was standing watch alone at the ship's bridge, reading. He had gone back to his beloved Shakespeare—the hell with them—when Magda appeared at his side.

"What are you reading?" she asked softly.

"The Taming of the Shrew," he replied, a bit more crisply than he had intended. It was not his favorite of Shakespeare's plays, but he knew it would really annoy Naomi if she found out.

"I always thought that one was pretty hilarious," she said.

"Not sexist?"

"Oh, definitely sexist, but you have to consider that Kate was played by an adolescent boy when it was first performed. It's still funny."

There was a brief, uncomfortable silence.

"Why did you say that the planet was at war?" she asked finally.

Ralph dropped his screen into his lap. "I was a fighter pilot for fifteen years before I joined the space program," he said. "And I could always tell when a region was hot. And I was always right. I'm not bragging, it's just an instinct you develop from experience."

"The others seem to feel that you don't respect them or their mission."

"Well, they're wrong. I do respect them, and their mission. I think Keith is an admirable and brilliant man, and I believe that he truly wants to do good. As does everyone on this ship. The problem is that they believe, sincerely believe, that everyone else feels exactly as they do. And that's a dangerous assumption. The kind that gets people killed."

Magda sat at the console beside him. "Tell me, Ralph. Why do your instincts tell you it's war? What tipped you?"

"Well, it was what *you* said. The bagpipe, coming through stronger than anything else. It was a forbidden instrument of defiance on our planet for centuries. All the other music was on what I guess are normal commercial frequencies. Not this one; someone wants to get the bagpipe out as far as it'll transmit. It's a signal, a rallying cry. I'm sure of it.

"Then the chemical emissions, and the guarded frequencies with a hell of a lot of traffic. It's a war, Magda, maybe a war of rebellion. And if it isn't a war, then there's something terribly wrong down there. Don't ask me how I know—I just know."

The navigational system emitted a buzz. "We're in the pipe," he said. "We've entered their solar system. Okay, six planets that I can see . . ."

Magda accessed the databanks. "Yes, they're the second planet from the sun, about 85 million miles away, but their sun is smaller than ours. What are you doing?" she asked, as Ralph laid in an alternate course.

"Their sun is between us and them. It may be smaller than ours, but we don't know anything about its gravitational pull. So what I'm doing is, we're gonna skirt the edge of their system and go the long away around. It won't take too much longer. See if comms are any clearer."

Magda placed her hand over her earpiece as she went through the channels. "A little bit stronger . . . wait." She laughed in surprise. "I think they've gotten our package!" she exclaimed. "Listen!" She switched the sound to overhead.

It was unmistakable; Mozart's *Eine Kleine Nachtmusik* issued clearly from the speaker.

"They're asking us in!" Magda said. "It has to be a signal of welcome!"

"Okay," Ralph said cautiously. "Maybe. Or . . ."

"Or what?"

"Maybe they just *like* it."

TWO weeks later, the *Lifespring* entered the planet's orbit.

All members of the crew stood assembled at the bridge as the ship established its automatic flyover of the planet's equator.

It was a moment charged with emotion. Eyes were wet and throats were lumpy. Only one hundred and thirty years before, the Wright brothers had made the first powered flight. And now, contact was about to be made with another world.

Ralph's hand was poised over the gate—if anything went wrong, the ship would blast out of orbit in a twinkling.

"Open the channel," Keith said, his voice cracking.

"Channel opened," Ralph replied.

Naomi and the rest of the crew joined hands.

"This is the Earth ship *Lifespring*," Keith began haltingly, fighting to check his emotions. "We have come in peace from the planet Earth."

No answer.

"We come in peace," he repeated.

Nothing.

"Our mission is a peaceful one."

Zip.

"Maybe they don't understand," Harry said.

"You'd think they'd say *something*," Naomi remarked, "whether they understand or not. I mean, how many extraplanetary visitors do they ever get?"

"Um," Keith began, "what's the name of your planet? We don't know what to call you."

Silence.

"Look, we don't want to bother you or anything, but we just want to make contact, that's all."

Zero.

"Look, this is a big thing for us!"

Static burst forth from the overhead speaker. *"Attention, Lifespring,"* a metallic voice began. *"This is the nation of Vidare of the planet Kivlan. We hope that this translation through our communications bank is sufficient."*

There were murmurs from the crew as they assimilated this new knowledge.

"Yes! Yes, it is!" Keith cried. "It's wonderful!"

"Good. That being established, we congratulate you on your achievement," the dull emotionless voice continued, *"and Godspeed to you all."*

"Godspeed," Harry noted. "They're a deistic peo—"

"We thank you for your interest and now request that you leave our orbit at once. May your journey home be free of peril."

"What!" Naomi exploded. "I don't believe it!"

Keith made shushing motions at her that he knew he'd pay dearly for later.

"Um . . . can we ask why?"

"Kivlan . . . declines extraplanetary contact at this time."

"Uh . . . why?"

"That is all. Oh. Thank you for your package. It was quite illuminating."

"Um . . . could we have something of yours—"

"That is all." The computer voice, though flat, was final. *"Please exit our orbit at once. This is your last friendly warning."*

"What do you mean by 'friendly'?"

The ship was suddenly jarred off its axis.

"A near miss," Ralph said calmly. "Some kind of high-energy blast. I'm initiating hull analysis."

"What the hell was that," Keith shouted.

"Your first unfriendly *warning,"* the voice replied, and electronic as it was, Keith swore there was a smirk behind it.

"Keith!" Ralph said sharply. "I'm getting us the hell out of here now!"

"Wait! Goddamn it, just wait!" Keith took a few seconds to calm down, but they weren't enough.

"Look," Keith said, "is there someone else we can talk to?"

Another explosion rocked the ship, much closer this time.

"Look, if you shoot us down, there'll just be more ships out looking for us. They know where we are. Are you gonna shoot them down, too?"

"The next one will not miss, Lifespring."

"Enough is enough," Ralph said, as he "busted the gate," enabling him to shove the throttles to full burn. The *Lifespring* left Kivlan's orbit in an eyeblink.

"*Bastards!*" Keith shouted.

TWO

ALEX Rayne was having one of the best days of his life, but he tried hard to keep his excitement under control as he addressed the UN Space Exploration Committee.

The former NASA director of Flight Operations tried hard to affect a stern countenance as he faced the committee, most of whom hadn't a clue of what he was talking about.

". . . it is therefore our finding that further voyages must be crewed—and commanded by—those with experience. Military experience. If you have reviewed the tapes, and I have many times, you can see that a tragedy was averted only in the nick of time. For it was the only military officer on the ship, Commander Ralph Jordan, who was able to keep cool in an extreme crisis. This is not meant to cast any aspersions on the other members of the crew; it is merely that Commander Jordan's training left him the only crew member truly prepared for such a contingency.

"It is also our belief," he continued, "that as painful a decision as it is, the world, nay"—he paused, asking himself if he had actually used the word *nay*—"the universe, is not the friendly and welcoming place we had hoped, and therefore our next ship must be, albeit defensively, armed."

There was an explosion of protests from the committee. Rayne gloried in it, anticipating with gusto the sentence he would utter next.

"Of course," he began, "it's up to you, but if this condition is not met, the United States will be forced to withdraw from the program." Boo-yaw! he exulted silently, get the money from someplace else, suckers!

And with that he nodded politely, gathered his papers, and left the room. Oh, yes, he thought, I'm back!

COMMANDER Ralph Jordan, resplendent in his dress whites, stood waiting for Alex Rayne as he emerged from the committee chambers. The two exchanged not a word as they descended to sublobby level in the elevator, but Ralph could tell from Alex's barely contained glee that the meeting had gone his way.

They exited at the lower-level coffee shop, which was still furnished with the same old wooden chairs and linoleum tabletops that Ralph had first seen as a schoolkid on a field trip.

"I always think of Bob Hope whenever I come here," Ralph said, when they had settled in with their coffee. "Movie I saw on TV when I was a kid—"

"A Global Affair," Alex replied.

Ralph nodded in surprise. "Yeah. It's always gonna be 1964 to me whenever I'm in this place," he said, "even though that was long before I was born. So, I take it, everything went well."

Alex held up his hand and bent his wrist as if he were shooting a basket. "Swish! We're back in business, kiddo. I'm gonna need you on this, Ralph."

Ralph made a forward pushing motion with his hands.

"Not me, pal. I'm going back to the Fleet."

"Ralph! No! You're going to command the next one. We need you, you've been there. Come on, I'll even get the Navy to throw in a fourth stripe."

"The hell with a fourth stripe. I'm going back to sea, where things make sense. I'll spend my days tripping the number-three wire, keeping the Indian Ocean or the South China Sea or wherever the hell safe for democracy, and my nights in my sea cabin, reading any damn thing I want. And every three or four months, I'll return to the warm and waiting arms of the woman I love."

Alex was taken aback. "You? The original confirmed bachelor? When the hell did this happen?"

"When I got back. Her name's Magda, she's a bio-chemist. Also a classical pianist with the voice of a—"

"You're a wild-assed fighter jock! A classical pianist?"

"It wasn't the piano. I heard her sing. It was on the ship, on the way home. Didn't even know the song, never heard it before. You know me, I like opera almost as much as I like shopping for wicker. But I heard her sing, and whammo, a big cartoon mallet hit me smack on the bean. Nothing happened in space," he added quickly. "It was after we landed. Never even asked her for a date. Just gave her a rose and my house keys."

"And she said yes, just like that?"

"Just like that. Ain't life a split-finger fastball?"

"God," Alex breathed. "What was the song?"

" 'Il Trutina,' from the *Carmina Burana*," Ralph replied.

"I can see that," Alex replied, playing the haunting melody in his head. "Done right, yeah, you could fall in love. Well, your life's taken care of. But did you ever think of me? Now that we've got the space program back where it belongs, out of the hands of the *Hi! Let's Hate America and on Its Own Soil, Too, Club*, what do I tell the president?"

"I'll help you with crew selection, Alex. I don't ship

out for another month. I'll consult on the ship specs. But that's it. *Finito*. I must go down to the sea again, old buddy."

Alex glanced shrewdly at his old friend. "What's really bugging you about this, Ralph?"

"I've got a bad feeling about it, Alex. These people, the ones on this planet, Kivlan."

"What about them? Don't you want to be the first—"

"No," Ralph cut him off. "I don't want to be the first. Or the second. Or the one thousand and eighty-fourth. These people—"

"What's wrong with them?"

"They're bright. They're obviously advanced. Scrapings from the hull of the ship, where we had that near miss, showed an energy concentration so high it was off the scale. And yet, something tells me they're not so different from us. But, and I can't shake this feeling . . . they're *nuts*."

I'VE served four presidents, Alex mused as he was ushered into the Oval Office, and not one of them would I trust to valet-park my car. I sure hope this one is different.

"Alex." The president of the United States rose and greeted him warmly, although they had never met before. "How're Kate and the kids?"

"Ah," Alex replied with an amused grin, "you've been well briefed. I'm flattered."

The president of the United States threw her well-coiffed brunette head back and gave her trademark infectious laugh. It was a charming, wicked, and decidedly sexy laugh, and hadn't hurt her public image in the least, although if it had, it would have been mitigated by a highly distinguished career in the U.S. Senate. She had been elected by the largest plurality in fifty years.

She motioned for him to sit in one of the two facing sofas and then settled in opposite him. "Coffee?"

"No thank you, Ms. President," he replied. Immediately after her election, President Ann Catesby had decreed that she would be called "Ms." as opposed to "Madame." "You don't call a male president 'Monsieur,' do you? So why in the hell should I be called 'Madame'?"

"I'm coffeed out from the flight, Ms. President," Alex said. "And I know your schedule is tight—"

"I'll worry about my schedule, Alex," she replied firmly. "Now play straight with me. Why in heaven's name should I risk seven lives and billions of American taxpayer dollars to establish contact with a planet that's already told us to take a flying leap?"

Well, all right, Alex thought approvingly. This lady has her head on straight. I'm glad I voted for her. "There is no reason, ma'am," he replied frankly. "In all honesty, there is no logical reason to continue. Except that we hold the franchise on space travel on this planet. The French, the Japanese, and the Russian programs are to service their satellites, but not to explore. There is no threat from anywhere else in that arena."

"What about a European consortium? They could well afford it. And they have the launch facilities on French Guiana."

"They could afford it, but they'd still need our expertise and at least our training facilities. And even then, what would be the point? Ten, perhaps fifteen billion dollars down a rathole, no profit to be made at the other end. What for? Just to say they did it?"

"You've answered your own question, Alex, but not mine."

"Ma'am, space travel is what America *does*. It's who we are, who we've been for the last eighty years. There's a world out there to be discovered, and it's our job to do it. Not the UN—they can barely keep *this* planet under control. It's just not their line of country, but it is ours. Because it's there. Unless we want to end up like Portugal."

"You've lost me, Alex. Portugal?"

"Go back to the early fifteen hundreds, ma'am. It was Portugal who led the world in exploration and discovery. She was a world leader. Her ships spanned the newly discovered globe and opened trade routes that made everybody rich. And then what happened? The Inquisition came in and shut it all down. That was the last time Portugal was ever a world power."

"You mean to say that we'll no longer be a world power if we don't toddle off to some hostile planet billions of miles away?"

"No. I'm saying that America is the leader of the free world. Everything that we do, we must do *first*. Ms. President, you know as well as I do that leadership is really little more than a sophisticated con game. It always has been, and always will be. People follow you because you can create that invincible aura of competence and control—and if you can't, they tell you to take a hike and they follow someone else. When we launch a ship off the pad and into deep space, we're saying that we're so cocksure that we have things down here under control, *of course* we're free to explore outer space. That's what America is for."

The president leaned back and stared thoughtfully out the window.

"All right," she said, finally, as she faced him again, "let's say, for the sake of argument, that I accept your proposal. How do you proceed? What's next?"

Alex suppressed a powerful urge to jump up and shout *yes!* The door-to-door salesman had just been admitted into the house and given a glass of water, the toughest part of any cold call. Now making the sale was entirely in his hands.

"The ship is a good one, ma'am," he began. "We have only to refit it, not replace it. More powerful engines, defensive laser shielding, and, of course, armament."

"What kind of armament?"

"Guns, ma'am; retractable, swivel-mounted thirty-millimeter Vulcans, and maybe some rockets. Ship to ship only, in case they come out to fight. If fired on from the planet, the ship is to leave the area immediately—there will be no air-to-ground capability."

"I'm glad to hear that," the president replied sternly. "We weren't invited—we'd have no business firing on their planet. None whatsoever." She turned to him with the face of the most powerful person in the world. "Is that understood?"

"Oh, yes, ma'am," Alex replied quickly.

"Now, the crew. In command, I want the best you've got. No nepotism, no politics, no next in line; the best. And *not* a cowboy. Someone who goes by the book. Is *that* understood?"

"Of course, Ms. President."

"One other thing. We're going to catch a lot of heat from the UN, so I want the XO and at least one more crew member to be from the European Consortium."

Alex winced. "One other crew member, fine, ma'am, but the XO? The second-in-command? Are you sure?"

The president looked at Alex as though he had just cursed in church.

"As you say, ma'am. It'll be taken care of."

"Why, thank you, Alex," she replied, rising. "Well, this is all very exciting! Do give my best to Kate and the children, won't you?"

THREE

THE USS *Harry Truman* pitched and rolled in the swells of the South Pacific Ocean. A warm trade wind blew down the carrier deck, refreshing the crew and giving the pilots an extra few knots of safety.

The captain nudged Alex Rayne and pointed at a pair of landing lights in the distance.

"There's CAG," the captain said. "He'll be on board in a minute."

Alex looked through borrowed binoculars at the approaching F-37 fighter.

"He's green all the way," the captain remarked, monitoring the landing signals officer's transmission with the incoming plane.

In another moment there was a painfully loud whine of engines and a bone-jarring thump as the commander air group's plane touched down and caught the number three wire for a textbook landing.

"Another three-wire landing for the CAG," the captain

said. "Ho-hum. I wonder if he even bothers to keep his eyes open."

Alex was escorted down to the deck by the Marine guard who had been assigned to him for the length of his stay. He reached the deck just in time to meet CAG as he pulled off his helmet.

Jesus, the guy even looks the part, Alex thought in wonder. His hair was dark and crew cut, his jaw was squared, his eyes a clear blue. He was tall and carried himself ramrod straight. Right out of Central Casting. He could already hear the brief conversation in his head; yes, sir, right away, sir, where and when do I report, sir?

"Captain Wiener?" Alex greeted him.

The stern face of command gave way to an easy grin. "You must be Mr. Rayne," he said, extending his hand. "Matt Wiener."

"Captain. That was one perfect landing."

"I'm scared to death every time I do it," Wiener replied.

"I'm sure that's an exaggeration."

"Well," Wiener shrugged modestly, "maybe a little. How can I help you, Mr. Rayne?" he added, raising his voice as another jet screamed onto the deck. "Why don't we get off the deck and go somewhere a little quieter?"

The labyrinthine hike to the ready room gave Alex the opportunity to reflect on Wiener's record. Born Newport Beach, California; straight-A student, Eagle Scout, and three-letter athlete; Annapolis, Class of '14, first out of 512. Doctorate from Cal Tech, aerospace technology. Superior ratings throughout his career. Joined the space program just before it was taken over by the UN, two deep-space voyages, one in command, both perfect. Returned to the fleet amid what was almost a bidding war for his services. He was just one of those guys who did everything better than everyone else; every Academy class had one.

On a personal note, the CAG was divorced, two children in college. No serious involvements at the moment.

When they reached the ready room, the Marine guard took up station near the door, CAG took a seat in the first row, and Alex sat on the desk in front.

"I suppose you know why I'm here, Captain," Alex said.

"Call me Matt, please."

"Fine. I'm Alex."

"The scuttlebutt, Alex, is that you're looking for a crew to go up again."

"That's right. What do you say?"

"Do I have a choice?"

"Why wouldn't you?"

"Never turn down a chance to volunteer, isn't that what they say, Alex?"

"Matt, I'm offering you command. Looking at your record, I'd say you're almost too good to be true."

Matt gave out a brief sardonic chuckle. "Well, it's been my experience that when they say you're too good to be true, you're not. Alex, I just work very hard to get things right. I always have. None of this came easily to me. But I wanted to fly, and now I do. I'm happy. All I ever wanted was to be a CAG. And now I am one. Why would you take that away from me?"

"Because the President told me to get the very best for the job, and that's you." Alex was uneasy; he had thought that Matt would jump at the offer, either out of a sense of duty or just plain desire. Instead he was making it plain that his arm would have to be twisted.

Matt yawned and stretched. "What are you offering me if I take it?"

"You're on a steady career path toward flag rank," Alex said. "You even aced Staff College. All you have to do is stay upright and relatively sober and the next promotion board will rubber-stamp it."

"Very well. So, what do I need *you* for?"

"You don't. But I need you. I need someone who won't

screw this up. 'Never refuse a combat assignment,' remember?"

"Combat? Nobody said anything about combat."

"Corporal?" Alex nodded at the Marine, who silently left the ready room and shut the hatch behind him. "Matt, our guys were fired on from the planet. They tried to make contact and the planet comms told them to get lost. When they didn't, there was a shot across their bow."

"So? Go find life somewhere else. Leave these people alone."

"It doesn't work that way, Matt. This is the only life-sustaining planet within our flight capability. Anywhere else would have to wait until a new propulsion technology for the engines is discovered. And we don't have the time."

Matt leaned back and yawned again. "But, Father, I don't want to go back to Harvard. I want to tap-dance on Broadway, see my name up in lights."

"This isn't you, Matt. This doesn't sound like one of the Navy's finest officers. Why are you being such a hard-case?"

Matt leaned forward and glared penetratingly at Alex. It was a withering stare; any creeping doubts about Matt's command fitness were suddenly blown away as if by a gale-force wind.

"I've given everything to the Navy and the space program. And that's okay; that's why I'm here and not on Wall Street or in some law firm in Century City. But my last voyage, my command voyage—the one that lasted a year. Do you know what happened when I came home? Or when I was away, to be technically accurate? My wife fell in love with someone else. Not that I blame *her*, you understand. Why should I? I was away more than I was home. The things that made me fall in love with her—*of course* they would make someone else fall for her, too."

Alex said, "Look, Matt, I'm sorry, but it happens. It's a fact of life in the service. You should—"

"I know all about that. But it's like car accidents—they're supposed to happen to the other guy, not me. Well, here's the news, Alex. When I promised to give my all for my country, that did not include my family. And that I cannot accept. So, I'm here, where I belong. I like being back in a fighter squadron. I get to fly all the time, there's the camaraderie, the macho nonsense, the satisfaction of doing an important job for my country in a highly specialized field. The ego boost of being part of an elite. But when I'm in port, I don't like being alone. I got married the day after I graduated from Annapolis; I don't like being a bachelor. There was a girl a while back, and she might have been the one, but both our jobs took us away from each other way too much. Well, that's not happening to me again. Next time *the* girl shows up, I'd like to be there to introduce myself."

God's sake, thought Alex. The best choice to command the first contact? This guy's still in high school!

Alex stood up. "Well, I'm sorry, Matt. You have no choice here. When you return, you'll be on the next All-Navy List for promotion to rear admiral and we'll get you command of your own task force. You can find another wife and live like a sultan in admiral's quarters. In or out, Captain. I can always get an executive order from the Oval Office. Of course, then the president would remember that she had to give you an executive order to go along."

"Don't bully me, Alex," Matt said wearily. "Many have tried, to their cost."

"All right, wait!"

"I knew I'd get it out of you eventually," Matt replied smugly.

"Get what out of me?"

"What's the real reason, Alex? Why is this so damned important? What're you afraid of?"

"All right, damn it! Okay, Matt, you're right, I wasn't as forthcoming as you deserved. I won't do it again. Now, this is the story. We made contact. They told us to take a hike. We didn't. They fired on us. So, here's the question: What if we got them really, really mad at us? What if they have a space travel capability far beyond our own, and they've decided that maybe we're going to be a problem for them? And what if they decide, let's get rid of this little problem before it becomes a big problem?"

"So, it's not really a wide-eyed and wonderful tear-jerking voyage of discovery, now is it, Alex? It's a god-damned preemptive strike!"

"No! I mean, not necessarily. You have to assess the situation and act—or not act—accordingly."

"Tell me I'm not going to be carrying nukes, Alex."

Alex smiled guiltily.

"You son of a bitch. The president agreed to this? I find that really hard to believe."

"Need-to-know basis, Matt. You're no stranger to that, are you?"

Matt grinned lopsidedly and shook his head. "I don't think I like you, Alex."

"Don't trust your first impression. I'll grow on you eventually. Report to Houston by twelve hundred hours on Thursday, Matt. It's nice having you on board."

ALEX'S next interview took place in decidedly more pleasant surroundings, at an outdoor café on the Champs Elysées. It was an obvious tourist trap that overcharged shamelessly, but the atmosphere made it well worth it.

Seated across from Alex, sipping a café au lait, was Jeanne-Marie Fournier, a coffee-break companion who in any other instance would have thrilled him. She was, to put it plainly, a knockout, exactly the sort of trés-chic, dangerously beautiful woman an American with precon-ceived notions would expect to see on Paris's most fa-mous boulevard.

But this was not any other instance. Jeanne-Marie Fournier was a commandant in France's *Armée de l'Air*, a skilled and highly-respected test pilot and the veteran of two voyages in space. She had been born in Senegal, but her parents had moved to France when she was a small child. She had graduated from St. Cyr, the French West Point, fifteen years before, and was rumored to be the mistress of a high-ranking cabinet member. This rumor was entirely untrue. The cabinet member had made a pass at her and was rebuffed. Jeanne-Marie's career was proceeding apace without any of *that* sort of help, thank you very much.

"Anyway, Major," Alex said, "you'll be the executive officer—second-in-command—and when you return you'll be—"

"Second-in-command?" Jeanne's English was astonishing. Two postgraduate years at Northwestern University in Chicago and a quick and sensitive ear had effectively given her English a flat Midwestern quality. Except, of course, when she was angry, like now—then her accent became heavily French again.

"*Second*-in-command?" she repeated. "Why am I not in command? Am I not qualified?"

"Oh, no, of course you—"

"Never mind! I know why! It is the American wallet that is dictating crew selection, not qualifications."

Alex tried to put his foot down—a big mistake. "Look, if that's the way you feel about it, you don't have to accept the mission—"

"Nonsense! Of course I must accept the mission! I am in the zone for promotion to lieutenant colonel. How can I ever expect to make general if I turn this down? If I turn anything down?"

"Major, you—"

"Very well, Monsieur Rayne," she said, calming down into an accentless English. "I will be your XO for this mission. And I will be a strong right hand for your Captain Wiener. We will visit this silly planet of yours and see to it that they behave. And if I return safely—"

"Major, that's not—"

"—*And if I return safely*, you will put a word in the ear of the marshal of the Air Force ensuring that I am retroactively promoted; that I am then to 'jump the zone' to full colonel; and that I am immediately accepted to General Staff College. Have we a deal, Alex?"

Without waiting for an answer, she gathered her clutch purse and rose from the table. "I expect to hear from you within the hour," she said, patting him on the shoulder as she passed him. "And if you cannot meet any one of my requirements, this conversation never took place and your offer never appears in my file. Enjoy Paris, Alex. The Tuilleries are lovely this time of year."

ALEX had only one choice for second officer and he instinctively knew that Major Claude Monroe would jump at the offer.

Monroe was the sort of success story that the military loves to brag about. Born in the Bedford-Stuyvesant section of Brooklyn to a crack-addicted teenage mother, Claude seemed destined for a short, violent life on the mean streets. A drug dealer making a thousand dollars a week by the time he was thirteen, Claude scratched and clawed his way to the near top of a brutal world. He wore gang colors, walked the walk, and carried a Tec-9 pistol that he held sideways when threatening a competitor. He was, as he later described himself, street vermin, fully resigned to dying in a glorious hail of gunfire at the hands of the police or another gang long before reaching the age of majority.

However, his career path took a sudden detour shortly before his eighteenth birthday. He was arrested in an undercover narcotics sting operation and held for questioning at the Brooklyn South precinct. And here a simple twist of fate changed his life forever.

One of the undercover cops had a brother in the Marines. The brother, home on leave, was on a ride-along with the cops when Claude was arrested. Captain Mark Hines immediately saw something in the young, defiant gangbanger as he watched his brother question him through the two-way mirror. The kid was charismatic and obviously bright; he had a crude and unpolished but undeniable gift for logic and rhetoric, and he easily deflected the cop's questions without appearing argumentative or intransigent.

Mark later took his brother aside and asked about Claude Monroe.

"Oh, hell yes, he's bright," Detective Frank Hines replied tiredly. "A lot of them are, that's what kills me. You can't get a bunch of brutal sociopaths to follow and obey you unless you have at least some intelligence. First time old Claude went up, they gave him an IQ test, and the guy's a total brainiac. It's a goddamned waste and it's *really* frustrating. I hate the little bastard, but I can't get over the feeling that I—that we, that I've—somehow failed him."

"Maybe not this time," his brother replied. "Can I have five minutes with him?"

"Mark . . ."

"Frank, look, the guy's gonna be dead within three years, probably sooner than that. Someone'll put a new hole in him. What's five minutes?"

His burnt-out brother shrugged wearily, which filled Mark with a deep sadness. Mark Hines had always idolized yet felt protective of his big brother. He had joined the Marines instead of the NYPD not only to step out from behind his brother's shadow, but also to avoid one day carrying the weight his brother was burdened with now.

"All right, Mark. It's his funeral."

"Maybe not," Mark replied.

Claude Monroe was completely disoriented. When the

door opened, he expected to see another cop. Why the hell were they sending in the Marines?

The big captain smiled. "Hiya, Claude," Mark greeted him heartily. "I'm Captain Hines. Pleased to meet you." And with that, he knocked Claude off his chair.

"Hey, what you doin'? You can't—"

"Well, actually, I can," Mark replied, picking Claude up by the collar of his silk shirt and jamming him back onto the chair. "Claude, I saw your file. You have an IQ of 148. I think you're gonna make one hell of a Marine."

"What!" Claude exploded. "I ain't joinin' no goddamn Marine—"

Claude found himself on the floor again in short order. "From now on, leave out the 'goddamns' when you talk about the Corps, Claude," Mark said, still smiling and friendly.

"You gonna help me up," Claude said sullenly.

"I don't know," Mark replied. "Depends on my mood. See what I'm saying, Claude? My life is filled with choices. Yours isn't. All you do is take up space. You're the boss of your 'crew,' but what are you the boss of? A bunch of surly lowlifes who are already dead and just haven't laid down yet. Your whole world is a few blocks of some ratty-assed slum. What a waste, Claude."

"It's my turf, man!"

Mark's smile was wide. "Not anymore, Claude. It's my turf now." He picked up Claude effortlessly and slammed him back in the chair. "I can go in there tomorrow, all by my lonesome, and take out everyone of you twerps if I feel like it. Don't even need a gun, just a piece of rope and maybe a knife. Do you doubt me?"

Claude kept silent. And once again, he was on the floor.

" 'Yes, sir; no, sir; no excuse, sir.' When you are asked a question, you answer, and that is what you say if you can't think of anything intelligent. Not answering at all is what's known as 'dumb insolence,' which is a monster no-no in the Corps. Okay, Claude?"

"Yes, sir," Claude said, after a long, tense pause.

" 'Yes, sir?' You mean you doubt me? You think I can't whack out every piece of crap gangbanger in your 'hood' anytime I feel like it? You really think your loser friends are any match at all for a Marine officer?"

"N-no, sir."

"Then why did you say so?"

"N-no excuse, sir."

"Claude, you're beautiful! I knew you'd get it!" He grabbed Claude's arm and lifted him. "Come on. Let's get outta here. We'll have a couple beers and I'll tell you all about your new life—the one that just got a whole lot longer."

FOR Claude Monroe, the rigors of boot camp were actually liberating. The pressure was off. No one was trying to gun him down every minute of the day and he realized in short order just how out of character the gangbanger life had been for him. He quickly emerged as a leader in his training platoon, and he found that he actually enjoyed having other people—real people, decent people, the sort he would have terrified but never thought would ever truly like or respect him—care for him and depend upon him.

He instinctively understood that the physical and emotional traumas visited upon him by the drill instructors were neither personal in nature nor done out of malice, and he was soon able to divine a glint of approval behind the harshness of manner.

Graduation day was an emotional passage for him. The Hines brothers were in the stands that day, and he wept unashamedly and with pride when each brother embraced him and Mark Hines told him, "The world is now yours."

Claude was sent to advanced recon training and received his high school general equivalency diploma during the cycle. A year later, Corporal Monroe went into battle for the first time, and was decorated for bravery far beyond the call of duty.

By now everyone wanted to help Claude Monroe, whose thirst for learning and advancement suddenly knew no bounds in this new world that conferred upon him a self-esteem that he never dreamed possible. He tested out of the first two years of college and was immediately selected for Officers Candidate School. Breezing through OCS at the top of his class, Second Lieutenant Monroe applied for flight training and in two years was a full-fledged fighter-bomber pilot. After six more years, during which time he had earned a master's degree and was halfway to his Ph.D., Monroe was selected for the space program.

It was just before joining the space program that an outrageously happy Claude Monroe decided it was high time that he found someone with whom to share his success. As with everything else in his life since joining the Corps, it happened as soon as he put his mind to it.

At Claude's wedding, Colonel Mark Hines took him aside and stared at him in wonderment.

"You know, Claude, I always knew you'd do okay in the Corps," Mark said. "Even when you were just a low-life gangbanger, I knew you'd get it together if you just used your head. But you amazed even me. You made it through boot camp at the top and joined a recon platoon, fine. You distinguished yourself in combat, even better. You go to college, unbelievable. Become a pilot, an astronaut! Hey, anything was possible for you, once you busted loose. But this, this is the goddamned, ever-loving end!"

Claude chuckled, knowing what was coming next.

"I mean, Claude," Mark said, "I can live with all that. And I'll take some credit for it. But this? I never thought, when I first slapped you around in that police station, not for one millisecond did I ever suspect that you were the son of a bitch who was going to wind up marrying my daughter!"

"MAJOR Monroe, I suppose you know why I'm here."

"I'll be in Houston in the morning, sir," Claude Monroe replied.

"Well, thank you, Major. I'm glad to finally meet someone who's gung-ho about this mission."

Claude Monroe regarded Alex with amusement.

"If that's what you think, sir—"

"Oh my God," Alex sighed, sounding for all the world like the exhausted Detective Frank Hines after a drug bust. "What *is it* with everybody?"

"Sir, I've been a Marine for twelve years, and in that time I've fought in brush wars, 'police actions,' and deeply misguided 'humanitarian' efforts. I've won a few, and I've had my butt beat. And there's been something consistent in every loss: It was in a place where we weren't wanted.

"Well, sir, you are sending us to a place where we are most assuredly not wanted. We will be lightly armed and sent in with an ambiguous brief. That, sir, is a virtual blueprint for defeat."

Alex stared in surprise at the brilliant, accomplished, and recruiting-poster-handsome Marine. It was hard to believe that this officer had ever been a drug-dealing gangbanger.

"Then why, Major? Why are you accepting this mission?"

Major Claude Monroe drew himself to a seated attention and allowed himself a tiny grin.

"The same reason that has driven me ever since the day I left the streets behind me and joined the Corps, Mr. Rayne. I'm *needed*."

FOUR

THERE would be seven members of the crew for the next voyage to Kivlan, but the command staff consisted of only three: Matt Wiener, the captain; Jeanne-Marie Fournier, the first, or executive, officer; and Claude Monroe, the second officer. If Matt were killed or captured, Jeanne would take over. If she met the same fate, Claude would succeed her. But if anything happened to Claude, the crew was to immediately abort the mission and return home.

Matt therefore believed that his first duty as captain was to bond with his XO and second officer as soon as possible. Not only to make the voyage smoother, but to present a united front against the administration, should it come to that.

Matt had subleased a luxurious apartment in a high-rise in Houston's Galleria district, a pied-à-terre for a patriotic solar energy baron who had long since become more at home in the rarified social circles of New York, Palm Beach, Bel Air, and Cannes. The deeply discounted apartment lease also included the services of a maid and a cook, and Matt Wiener, who in the back of his brain held the conviction that he wasn't coming back from Kivlan, enjoyed making what could possibly be his last days on his home planet a sumptuous experience.

He had therefore invited Jeanne and Claude to dinner on their first night together in Houston. Dinner was a quiet, almost desultory affair, with conversation inhibited by the presence of the two retainers.

It was only when the dinner was cleared away and the maid and cook were dismissed for the night that the three felt comfortable enough to talk. They stretched out on the sofas near the fireplace with their cognacs when Matt addressed them seriously for the first time.

"We've got a problem, boys and girls," Matt pronounced.

"You've got that right," Claude replied.

"I think we've more than one," Jeanne said.

"Let's get the minor one out of the way," Matt said. "Alex Rayne told me that in the same way that the UN wanted any evidence of military involvement erased from the program, they now want any traces of 'enviroloonyism,' his word, removed from this one. Hence, the name *Lifespring* is now history. As captain, the privilege of renaming the ship falls to me. But I want your involvement in this. It's your ship, too."

"How about the *Andrea Doria*?" Claude suggested.

"Why not the *Lusitania*?" Jeanne countered.

"Why not the *Titanic*?" Matt retorted. "Am I missing something here?"

"Doomed ships," Claude said morosely. "Sorry. You're right, Matt, I apologize. That attitude is unacceptable." He paused and thought for a moment. Then he brightened. "How about the *Forlorn Hope*?"

"Oh, that is a great improvement," Jeanne scoffed.

"Actually," Claude began, "it's not as off the mark as you'd think. 'Forlorn hope' is a military term, used by the British circa the Napoleonic Wars."

"The British . . ." Jeanne grunted out of national pride.

"The forlorn hope," Claude continued, "was what they called the advance guard sent out to gain a foothold on enemy ground, which would then be reinforced and exploited by following troops. Isn't that really what we're doing?"

"Hmm," Matt replied interestedly. "The *Forlorn Hope*. To tell you the truth, I like it. Yes, I believe I do." He shook his head dismissively. "But they'd never buy it. Sounds too pessimistic."

"Let us think," Jeanne said, "and dispense with this . . . creeping Anglophilia. You spoke of our attitude. What is our attitude? Should we not define that first?"

"Very good, Jeanne," Matt said approvingly. "And that is the reason I called you here. Vietnam, Somalia, Bosnia, Belarus, Uganda—all doomed missions with no real objectives. The kind of political bungling that accomplishes nothing and gains nothing but fresh plots at Arlington. So, children, let's decide *now*. Why do you think they're sending us to this planet?"

"Because they're afraid," Jeanne replied firmly. "We have awakened the sleeping tiger, and they fear he will spring."

"And what is our brief? Claude?"

"We have to determine just how angry this tiger is. Is he now going to come after us? Is he just preoccupied with matters at home, and maybe we just caught him on a bad day? Maybe he really does want to be friends." Claude paused. "Or maybe he wants to make sure that we never bother him again."

"Matt," Jeanne asked. "I saw the specs for the refitting. I noticed that a storage area has been reconfigured for filtered isolation. That could mean only one thing."

"I was going to tell you," Matt said miserably.

"We know," Jeanne replied.

"Nukes," Claude said. "They really expect us to nuke the planet if they piss us off?"

Matt couldn't say anything. All he could do was nod.

"Are we going to?"

Matt thought for a moment, and a slow smile crossed his face. "It occurs to me—and Jeanne, I hope you'll forgive me—we just might have them by the short ones."

"Oh?" Claude replied.

"Oh?" Jeanne replied.

"Yes! The impression I get is, the president told Alex no nukes. If Kivlan sends up a ship to attack us, we can defend ourselves. But we are not to attack the planet's surface. So, what happens? Alex smiles and says, 'Oh, indubitably, ma'am,' and proceeds to stock the ship with nukes anyway. I'll bet a year's pay that one of our yet-to-be-selected crew members is going to be a ringer from the Navy or Air Force Nuclear Division. Any takers? Didn't think so."

Matt freshened up snifters all around.

"Now, I say this, and tell me if you agree: If we are attacked by a ship, we blast it. But if we are attacked surface to space, we book. So: Do we attack the planet? No matter what happens, under any circumstances. . . . Did we join the space program to discover new worlds or to destroy them? Once again: Do we nuke the planet, orders or not?"

Claude stood up. "No. No way."

Jeanne stood up. "Not under any circumstances, not at all."

"Then we're decided. It's our ship, our rules, our name." Matt raised his glass. "Jeanne. Claude. Welcome. I give you the command staff of GASA's—correction, NASA's—newest ship. I give you . . . the *Forlorn Hope*."

ALEX Rayne did not like the name *Forlorn Hope* at all, being largely unschooled in history and therefore unable to grasp its subtlety.

"It sounds like a last-ditch, desperate effort," he complained.

"Tough," Matt said. "I like it. We like it. Captain's privilege, the name stays."

"The public won't buy it."

"They won't be flying it, either."

"Look, I'm not saying it has to be touchy-feely-save-the-rain-forest like *Lifespring* was, but can't you at least come up with something a little less . . . I don't know."

"No," Jeanne said flatly.

"*Forlorn Hope,*" Claude said proudly.

"Because that's what we're telling the media, anyway," Matt added. "Either that," he said, grinning at Claude, "or we call it the *Whale-Saving Enviroweenie.*"

"Okay," Alex sighed. "*Forlorn Hope* it is."

THE ringer Alex Rayne had chosen to oversee the ship's nuclear-strike capability was the only astronaut in the program who was not a pilot at all, not even logging the required ten hours of jet time usually needed to qualify for space flight.

Navy Lieutenant Bob Rodgers had never had anything whatsoever to do with flying, which was fine with him. Not only because he always became airsick but also because despite the fact that he was a brilliant nuclear physicist, he never could understand how it was even possible that hundreds of thousands of pounds of metal could get off the ground and not fall down. His extraordinarily keen mind could confirm it theoretically, but his heart couldn't even credit the possibility.

Bob Rodgers had graduated from MIT on the Navy's ROTC program, the only way he could have possibly afforded college. The son of a dirt-poor farmer and lay preacher from Mississippi, Bob Rodgers saw the Navy's Nuclear Power Reserve Officer Candidate Program as his only way out of the mud and the bleak and cheerless upbringing that had been his early life. He was fortunately quick in his studies, especially at math and science, and when the regional Navy recruiter, who had called upon the local high school's valedictorian on the hunch that college was financially a pipe dream, Bob all but fell gratefully into his arms. Bob easily qualified for a Navy scholarship and left home without ever looking back.

Bob fell in love with the Navy. Not because of any particular affinity for the military life, although it was ultimately far less strict than his own puritanical upbringing, but because the Navy just never stopped giving. Its generosity never ceased to amaze him through his entire undergraduate career. It was as if he had discovered a kindly rich relative who was guiltily trying to make it up to him after years of neglect. All he had to do was excel in his studies, go to officers training camp every summer, and promise a year on active duty for every year of education the Navy underwrote. In return, the Navy not only paid for his tuition, room, board, computer, software, and books, but also, for gosh sakes, paid him a *salary*, even during the school year, when the closest he ever got to anything nautical was watching the Harvard crew team sculling on the Charles River. He didn't have to take a part-time job, which surprised him, and was even able to buy a car, which absolutely floored him.

Bob graduated with honors and set about paying the Navy back for the last four wonderful years. Despite his relief at being set free from his childhood and given a place in the world, his rigid upbringing had instilled him with certain virtues and values, and he told his Navy career counselor that he would go wherever the service needed him the most. Because nuclear engineers do not, as a general rule, grow on trees, the Navy deemed him a valuable commodity and sent him off to New London, Connecticut, for submarine training.

For the next eight years, Bob Rodgers served with dedication and distinction on both sea and shore. He was considered a definite comer in the service, one who was certain to proceed steadily up the ranks toward eventual command of his own boat—if private industry didn't snap him up first.

Naval officers generally served two years at sea and two years in a shore billet. Rodgers used shore duty to expand his educational credentials, but having already received his doctorate in his previous stint on land, he was determined to dedicate the next shore assignment exclusively to the pleasant process of finding himself a wife. That was when he received a call from Alex Rayne to report to Houston at once. This assignment, he was assured, would not be a deviation from his career path toward command; in fact, it was entirely possible that if he acquitted himself honorably, he just might find himself in line for the next XO vacancy in the subfleet when he returned to sea—which would put him an unheard-of four years ahead of the game.

"Of course, Mr. Rayne," Bob Rodgers said into the phone. "I'll be happy to do whatever is required."

THERE now remained only the selection of two mission specialists and the flight surgeon. Because the voyage would be so long in duration and take the crew so far from any medical facility, a fully accredited surgeon was required on board to handle all medical contingencies from paper cuts to open-heart surgery.

The choice was obvious to the crew and became unanimous. Air Force Lieutenant Colonel Doralee Conger-Levin, at fifty—three years older than Matt Wiener— would be the oldest crew member aboard the *Forlorn Hope*.

There was good reason for her unanimous acceptance by the three command officers. Not only was Dr. Conger-Levin a cardiologist highly esteemed both in and out of the service, but she was also one of the kindest and most likable people any of them had ever met.

Like Bob Rodgers and Claude Monroe, Doralee Conger was born into debilitating poverty. Unlike Claude and Bob, she stood to become a helpless victim of it very early on in life.

Born in a small, economically long-dead town in West Virginia to an alcoholic father and a weak-minded mother, Doralee was three when her loving but otherwise useless father died of complications brought on by acute alcholism. Her mother, desperately afraid of being alone, brought a succession of men into the house, most of whom were violent and frightening and constantly told Doralee she was stupid. Doralee was sexually abused beginning at an early age; it became worse as she progressed through adolescence and showed signs of developing into the very pretty woman she would become. She married young to escape, and soon found that she had merely jumped from the fire into another fire. Her husband told her she was so stupid she was worthless, and beat her regularly until the day he simply walked out the door never to return, leaving her penniless and alone.

With nowhere else to go, nineteen-year-old Doralee wandered into an Army recruiting station, hoping for little else than a free coffee and donut to quiet the pangs in her stomach. The recruiting sergeant took one look at Doralee and saw herself ten years before, which made her immediately take the defeated young girl under her wing. She sent out for a meal for Doralee and dropped the recruiting spiel completely. The girl was obviously sweet with a kindly nature, still able to project an outward innocence despite what she had already endured, and it almost broke the sergeant's heart when she thought of the fate that probably awaited her. The sergeant told Doralee of her own tragic early life, her equally brutal husband, and how he had left her in even worse shape than Doralee; she had two small children to feed, no education, and no choice but to go on welfare. On a desperate impulse she had joined the Army. Now, ten years later, she was halfway to a college degree; her children were growing up happy, strong, and healthy; and she had married again, this time to someone from the same species.

"The Army's made for people just like us, honey," the sergeant told her. "I mean, where else could po' white trash like us ever go? The Army's the only exit ramp off Tobacco Road."

Doralee joined the Army that very day, and twelve weeks later found herself a private second-class assigned to training as a medic. She served out her three-year enlistment and transferred to the Air Force, which she had been told could offer her a wider selection of technical careers.

She also made a realization that gave her something of a shock: No one had called her stupid or worthless since the day she became a soldier.

While working as a medical assistant in an Air Force hospital, a new commanding officer studying her record remarked that she was obviously bright; why didn't she try for a nursing degree? Doralee was flabbergasted; not only at the possibility that she could actually become a nurse, but because a *man*, who wanted nothing from her, had told her she was bright. She prepared intensively for the entrance exam and surprised no one but herself when she scored top marks. Having made that discovery, she made another, one all the more frightening because it had never seemed even worth thinking about before: What she really wanted was to be a doctor. It had been a childhood dream that she knew could never become a reality—to make sick people well, to stop people from suffering. But she was poor and stupid and believed she stood a better chance of becoming a princess.

Suddenly, the long-repressed dream broke the surface like a submarine blowing ballast, and loomed on the horizon as more than just the faintest of possibilities. And it scared her to death. It took days before the mere thought of it ceased to make her tremble in fear. And what made it all an even scarier prospect was the simple fact that, suddenly, it *was* possible. If she was smart enough to get into nursing school, then she was also smart enough to go pre-med; there was simply no getting around it. And even tuition, a word that had never even entered her vocabulary in her pre-service days, was no problem either; the Air Force would pay her way. All she had to do was study hard and work like hell. And that, she knew she could do. A girl who had been called stupid for most of her life was going to be a doctor!

It took her a long time, but twelve years after she first tried to enter nursing school, she received her medical degree, and began her residency in cardiology at the University of Miami Medical Center.

Half a career later, she was an astronaut and married to the world's most wonderful man, a respected cardiologist like herself. Not bad, she sometimes thought, for po' white trash, for somebody *stupid*; not bad at all.

UNLIKE Doralee Conger, Air Force Captain Hayes "Butch" Caldwell III came from a background so privileged one almost expected a rap on the door from a proletariat informing his folks that playtime was over.

Hayes Caldwell's family was an FFV, one of the Virginia aristocracy's oldest and wealthiest families. Even the Civil War had not destroyed the Caldwell fortune; a family wag in a later generation would paraphrase Henry Thoreau when explaining the endurance of the family's wealth: "Diversify, diversify."

Hayes Caldwell was the youngest of four brothers, all of whom were highly competitive overachievers. As the youngest, Hayes was often overlooked, which irritated him to no end. His only consolation was that his father had waited until he was born to confer his name on a son. That scant comfort was ingloriously stolen forever when he discovered that the births of his three older brothers were inconveniently preceded by the deaths of close relatives, whose names were respectfully passed on to the newest family members. The day little Hayes found this out, he demanded that everyone call him "Butch" from then on. No one knew where he had gotten the name Butch from, but it was the first time little Hayes's strong will ever asserted itself successfully, and he found that he enjoyed it. "Butch" he remained forever.

Butch spent much of his youth trying to break out of the mold his brothers fit into so successfully. While his brothers were football stars, young Butch lettered in soccer. Where his brothers won honors on the debating team, Butch starred for the drama club. His brothers became big men on campus at the University of Virginia, while Butch was a campus leader at the University of North Carolina. His brothers were family legacy pledges at Alpha Tau Omega; Butch joined Phi Delta Theta.

As men, Butch's brothers hated flying and never would have dreamed of entering the peacetime military; Butch joined the Air Force and became a fighter pilot.

Butch's parents didn't know what to make of their youngest son's choice of career. His father had even threatened to cut off his sizable trust fund if he didn't "stop fooling with this Air Force stuff and get a real job." Butch's response had been to touch his cap and say, "See ya." The threat was immediately retracted.

Six months later, it was announced that the space program was looking for pilots. Butch applied and was accepted. Three years later, Butch was selected as a crew member for the USS *Forlorn Hope*, the ship that would make first contact with another planet (the *Lifespring*'s failure having been hushed up by the UN). When the final crew selection was offically announced, its group photo was printed in every major newspaper in the world. No one in the offical photo looked prouder than Butch.

Butch went home and enjoyed the best Sunday dinner

he had ever eaten with his family in all of his thirty-one years.

LIKE Matt Wiener and Jeanne-Marie Fournier, Flight Lieutenant John Ryham had grown up in a family solidly entrenched in the middle class. Unlike them, he had joined the military to escape his former self.

A native of the London suburb of Bexley, John Ryham had been overweight as a child. His accountant father, desperately clinging to a dead-end, middle-management job that left him in mortal fear of redundancy every waking moment, had little time for his small family. His mother tried to make up for it by spoiling him, plying him with food and sweets in place of the understanding and self-esteem John really needed.

His childhood nickname, courtesy of his kind playmates, was Fat-fat-fatty. This was when they included him in anything at all. John became a tremulously nervous child, never knowing when the friendly verbal cruelty of his playmates would turn ugly and physical. He grew up feeling ashamed and foolish, afraid to try anything, knowing he would fail miserably and embarrass himself. By the time he was fourteen, he had been humiliated, or had humiliated himself, in every way possible for a schoolboy; by then even his teachers at the third-rate public school his father could barely afford had almost given up on him.

Like Claude Monroe and Doralee Conger-Levin, his life turned around on a simple whim of destiny.

It was his first train ride alone. He was being sent to his gran's house in Bournemouth for the summer holidays, and his father had to work as usual and told his wife that "if John can't handle an hour on the train by himself without cocking things up, he ought to for Christ's sake be traded in for another model."

So John sat alone in a second-class carriage watching the countryside roll by, nervously going through the bag of chocolates his mother had given him for the trip. Suddenly the door was thrown open and in stepped a fellow from right out of the movies. He was a wing commander in the Royal Air Force—John could tell that right away from the sky-blue uniform and the three rings on each sleeve. He was flight crew but not a pilot, probably a radar intercept/weapons officer; John knew that by the one wing attached to a silver bullet on his chest, where a pilot's wings would normally go.

Summoning up every ounce of courage he had, John extended the bag of chocolates to the wing commander. The wing commander nodded solemnly and accepted one from the bag.

"Caramels," the wing commander said, chewing. "Haven't had a caramel chocky in years. Thank you, my boy."

Before he could stop himself, John asked, "Please, sir, how does one become a pilot in the RAF?" He avoided the urge to screw his eyes shut for the inevitable answer when it came: "There's no place in the RAF for a fat tub of lard like you."

But to his amazement, the wing commander said no such thing. Instead his reply was, "Well, the first requirement, and certainly the most important, is that you have to be quite mad. A loony far beyond help. Anyone who spends their working day in forty thousand pounds of metal five miles high going six hundred miles an hour, looking for people to blow to kingdom come, can't be all there, now, can they?"

John stared in amazement. "I don't suppose so," he replied without even knowing it.

"Still, it's better than all this, isn't it, then? Popping off to some silly job in town, behind a desk with idiots yammering at you all day about things that ultimately don't matter a toss."

John thought of his father and agreed wholeheartedly.

"Please, sir," he said, "I think I might be mad enough."

"Well, good for you, son! How old are you?"

"Fourteen, sir."

"Ah! Bags of time, then. How are your grades?"

"Could be better, sir."

"I see. Make them better—no, make them the best. Then the physical. One hundred push-ups," the wing commander lied, not remembering for the life of him what the requirements were, "two hundred sit-ups, run three miles in the half hour. Piece of cake!"

John's heart sank. "Three miles," he asked, pained from the run already.

"Nothing to it, old boy. I was much fatter than you when I was your age," he added, lying through his teeth. "Absolutely," he said, warming to the fictive subject. "They used to call me Fuji-Blimp and Sumo-man."

The wing commander was tall and slim. No one had ever discussed John's weight so matter-of-factly and without judgment before, as if it were a trivial and temporary condition like a stomachache or a headcold, easily overcome and soon forgotten. "Really, sir?"

"Oh, yes. Look, you don't have to be able to do all those push-ups and things *tomorrow*, old fellow. Try one tonight, two tomorrow, and three the next day. I daresay by Christmas you'll be quite proud of yourself. Same with the running—I'm afraid there's no getting 'round that, old chap—just run a block today. Two tomorrow. By Easter you'll be like one of those Kenyans who always wins the American marathons. When you've done all that, shoot a letter off to the RAF College at Cranwell and let them know you're interested. I'm sure they'll be delighted."

It was an incident the wing commander promptly forgot the moment he alit from the train, but it was the turning point in John Ryham's life. *I'm sure they'll be delighted.* From that moment forward he envisioned himself as a tall and slim officer in the Royal Air Force. He arrived at his gran's in Bournemouth and immediately went for a run on the beach. He could make only fifty yards that first day, and just barely eke out two push-ups that first night, but his new obsession caught and took hold. Who do you want to be, he would urge himself, Fat-fat-fatty or Pilot Officer John Ryham, RAF? Tub o' lard or Squadron Leader Ryham, DFC? Whale-arse or Air Chief Marshal Sir John Ryham, KCB? And he would force out just one more push-up.

When he returned home that fall, his shocked parents took a renewed interest in their newly determined and fast-slimming son. He announced his intentions with such heretofore unheard-of conviction that his parents had no choice but to respect his ambition. They united behind him and all became much closer as a result. His father wrote away to Cranwell for the admissions guide and spent the next four years helping his son prepare mentally and physically for the grueling entrance exams. His mother consulted nutritionists and bought every diet book available to ensure that everything John ate from then on would give him energy and strength instead of comfort and calories. Four years later, he was admitted to the RAF College at Cranwell. At the age of twenty-one, he stood before the mirror a handsome, strong, and supremely confident young man in the uniform of a pilot officer in the RAF. Eight years later, when he heard the Yanks were recruiting foreign pilots for the space program, he jumped at it. He felt he owed it to the poor little fat kid.

MATT'S penthouse became the focal point of off-duty activity for the crew of the USS *Forlorn Hope*. After all, the crew would be living at close quarters for a year; it was better they learned each other's personality traits and quirks now, the better to deal with them in space.

Matt hosted frequent rooftop pool parties and barbecues for the crew and their families. Any or all of the crew were invited to his house for a drink after the working day. That was the ultimate responsibility of command,

Matt felt; a commander had to be available and accessible to his crew at any hour of the day and for any reason. The only exception was the week of college spring break when his children came down to visit him.

He had missed them terribly, and never forgave himself for not being there as they grew up. His wife and her husband had done a wonderful job with them, though; they were good kids with all the right values.

But it nevertheless shocked him when one evening after dinner they made an eye-opening admission.

"Daddy," his daughter Kim said frankly, "we don't want you to go."

"What?"

"Blow it off, Dad," his son David affirmed. "Tell 'em you've got a hernia or something, piles, Saint Vitus' dance, we don't care. Just don't go."

"Please, Daddy," his daughter begged.

"I don't get it," Matt said. "Aren't you proud of your old man? I'm going to be the first—"

"Of *course* we're proud of you," David cut him off. "But we're also scared to death you won't be coming back. So's Mom. She hasn't had a full night's sleep in weeks. She keeps dreaming about you, dead, floating around in space forever."

Matt was taken aback. He and his ex-wife would always like each other, but he had never realized that she still worried about him.

"I'm sorry," he said. "No, I truly am. But, kids, this is what I do. It's who I am. And to tell you the truth, space travel is a hell of a lot safer than a night carrier landing."

"Yeah, well, we were never too crazy about *that,* either," David said.

"David, a man can't run from who he is," Matt said.

"Oh, *puh-leeze*," his children groaned in concert. "Dad," Kim began, "didn't you have a girlfriend? Don't you want to get married again?"

"Yes and yes," he replied. "I *had* a girlfriend, she lives

in Washington, and I'm going to be away for a year, not that I was ever there much to begin with. And her career kept her even busier than I ever was. And yes, I do want to get married again. Very much. And when I meet the right woman, I'll do it first thing."

"But, Dad, this is so dangerous—"

"Kim's right," David said. "This isn't one of those missions where you fly around and do all kinds of boring experiments that nobody can understand anyway. This is the real deal, and no one knows what you'll be up against."

"Kids, listen to me," he began in a serious tone. "This is what I've wanted my whole life. It's what I always dreamed of. Growing up in Newport, I never would have believed it could happen to me. Neither would your grandparents. They thought I'd go to law school or get an MBA—and so did I, for a while. But I wanted to fly. And I thought, 'Why shouldn't I?'

"Guys, just wanting it wasn't enough. I had to work so hard! Much harder than if I had wanted to get into Harvard or Stanford. And I had to have the talent—which I did, fortunately. But so did lots of other guys, and I had to beat them all out to get appointed to Annapolis.

"Kids, this is what I do. It's who I am. And most importantly, it's exactly who I always wanted to be."

"Matt Wiener, Space Hero," David pronounced melodramatically. "For God's sake, Dad—please be careful."

"Please come back to us, Daddy," Kim urged him tearfully.

"Come here, both of you," Matt said, "group hug." The three embraced. "When I come back," Matt said with far more conviction than he felt, "I'll spend more time with both of you."

"Promise," his daughter asked.

"Just try and keep me away. I'll be a real pain in the butt, I promise."

FIVE

THE USS *Forlorn Hope* was far too large to be launched as the space shuttles had been—piggy-backed on a rocket. Three times the size of shuttle-class vehicles, the *Forlorn Hope* had to carry enough fuel and supplies for a fourteen-month voyage. Each crew member had their own space—tiny cubicles with pull-down beds and desks and video screens in the wall. Privacy, or at least a small measure of it, was required for a voyage of this duration.

The *Forlorn Hope* was therefore launched like a jet off a carrier, by what amounted to an explosive catapult. The ship would be blasted into space by exterior power only; then, once outside the Earth's orbit, the crew would "light the burners" and the ship would begin its voyage for real.

Matt had gotten into a shouting match with Alex Rayne over cameras in the cockpit during the launch. Alex believed that to show astronauts during the actual blast-off would be a public relations coup. Matt knew better; to be blasted off the face of the earth like shell from a cannon and then to immediately shoot "over the top," out of orbit and into weightlessness, was an emotionally and physically explosive experience. To hear the crew shrieking—out of exhilaration or fear or both—and to see them retching as it occurred, was nobody's damned business but their own. There were other disagreements as well, but Matt let most of them slide. Bob Rodgers had been fully accepted into the crew, but it was an emotional strain on the command staff to pretend they weren't aware of his real function.

And there were other things—small, seemingly inconsequential things that made everyone just short of crazy: the food selection, the choice of books available on personal reading units, crew games, even the brand of toilet paper (everybody wanted the soft stuff, but it weighed twice as much)—all of which seemed quite silly on the surface, but not for people who would have no other options for at least a year. All of these issues, large and small, made Matt Wiener's life difficult, but this was nothing: Three weeks before the actual launch, Captain Matt Wiener's life became infinitely more complicated.

The entire crew was flown up to Washington for a private audience with the president, the usual public relations claptrap. It was brief, lasting all of fifteen minutes, but it provided good fodder for the media.

Despite the honor of meeting the president, the trip was an unwelcome intrusion in the hectic schedule this close to the launch date. The crew was glad to get back to Houston that afternoon and pick up where they had left off in their preparations.

It had been an exhausting day for Matt Wiener, and when he arrived at his apartment late that night, all he wanted was to fall into bed. He was just about to drift off to sleep in his clothes when his bedside phone rang.

"Captain Wiener, I hope I haven't disturbed you."

"Who is this?' he asked drowsily.

"I think you know," the voice replied with a touch of amusement.

Matt became alert at once. "What can I do for you, ma'am?"

"There's a limo downstairs. Get in." The voice rang off.

Matt jumped into the shower and gave himself a quick washdown. Then he dressed quickly and took the elevator to the street. A limo was waiting as promised. Matt got in and the driver took off at top speed without saying a word. The limo roared up US 59 to Houston Interconti- nental Airport, where he was let off at a private hangar.

Two men in suits, wearing earpieces, scanned his body for weapons. Then he was ushered into a Gulfstream G-IX with the legend "United States of America" painted on the fuselage.

"How long will this take," he asked an Air Force stew- ard.

" 'Bout three hours, Captain."

"My tax dollars provide me with a shaving kit and a toothbrush?"

"Of course, sir."

"Wake me up in two and a half hours," he ordered. "Coffee light with a chemical, and the tallest glass of OJ you've got." Then he settled into the plush club seat and was asleep before he could fasten his safety belt. The steward had to do it for him.

It was deep in the Washington night when the plane touched down at Andrews Air Force Base. Matt was hus- tled off the plane and into a waiting sedan by Secret Ser- vice agents. In a very short time the sedan was admitted through the west gate of the White House.

It was disorienting to be in the Oval Office for the second time in one day; and even more so to be led into the president's private office.

There was a homey feel to the place, made all the more so by the many photos of the president's daughters, a sort of illustrated life story of the two girls from infancy to college.

"Matt, thanks for coming by," the president greeted him.

"I just happened to be in the neighborhood," he replied drily, not entirely unable to notice this was the only American president in history who filled out a pair of jeans so nicely.

"Let's have some coffee," the president said. "I need to talk to you, and I wanted it strictly between us." It was after three in the morning, and Matt wondered how the president could look so fresh and alert. He decided that power must be energizing.

She sat on a sofa and patted the cushion next to her. "I'm sorry to inconvenience you, especially now, but there's something we need to get out in the open."

"I understand," Matt said, knowing exactly what was coming. From the knowing look in her deep green eyes, the president knew that he knew.

"Does Alex Rayne think I'm an idiot?" she asked.

"That's a rhetorical question, isn't it, ma'am?"

"Matt. There are nukes on board, aren't there?"

Matt didn't hesitate. "Of course there are, ma'am."

"Is the rest of your crew aware of this?"

"My command staff, Majors Fournier and Monroe, knew immediately when they saw that the specs for the refitting included an isolation area. The rest of the crew— it's just a matter of time."

"I could shut down your whole program right now," she said. "Are you aware of that?"

"Right now, Ms. President, I really don't care. No one thinks this mission is that wonderful an idea. Even my kids have begged me not to go. My command staff and I have already decided our policy, since no else saw fit to do so. Those nukes stay where they are, stored and disarmed. We are not traveling billions of miles to blow up another planet."

"What about your nuclear officer? And don't tell me

there isn't one, or why would a submarine officer be drafted into the program?"

Matt stifled a yawn. "The word, for public consumption anyway, is that months of confinement in space is more like sub duty than aviation. I'll handle Rodgers when the time comes, but I'd like an official order from you. He's a good officer, but he's been put in a difficult position. I'd like to help him out."

"I'll give it to you before you leave. Well, that was easy." The president glanced at him sideways. "You look exhausted, Matt."

He smiled ironically. "I've had a long day." It suddenly occurred to Matt that the president might have called him to Washington for an entirely different reason. But how in the hell do you ask the *president* for a date?

"Ms. President—"

"Matt. If you call me that one more time, I'm going to smack you silly."

"This is not a good idea, Ann," he said.

She moved closer to him. "Why not?"

"Well, for one thing, I live in Houston, and you live in DC. We've just been through one of those, a G-U deal. Remember?"

" 'G-U?' "

"Geographically undesirable. And for the next year, starting in about three weeks, I'm gonna be about as G-U as all get-out."

"Matt. I haven't had a date in three years. If you don't count the prime minister of Italy putting his hand on my knee at a state dinner. I know you've been divorced a long time. Wasn't there anyone since me? Don't you want to get married again? I'm not proposing, mind you," she added quickly, "just asking."

"The truth? Sure I do. I'll make a little confession. I like all the macho things the Navy gives me. I like to think of myself as a man's man, and I don't apologize for it. But at home, in my own bedroom, I miss having someone with me, and I miss luxuriating in all of the warm frilly girly stuff my wife furnished the place with, the things *you* had. All those things that a guy would never have in his vocabulary if he stayed single his whole life— duvets, valances, pillow shams, et cetera. What about you?"

"Matt. Didn't you miss me, even a little?"

"I'd say more than a little. I'd say more than a lot. I wanted to call you a million times. And then you got elected *president*, for God's sake. I mean, it was one thing when you were a senator, even though you were high-profile, we still had a semblance of privacy."

"I'm still the same girl, Matt. And I still miss you."

"So what do we do?" Matt asked her. "Meet after work at TGI Friday's for a couple of margaritas? Hit the multiplex for a flick?"

"Why not?"

"Because you're the president."

" 'The king is but a man,' " she quoted, " 'his ceremonies laid by, in his nakedness, he appears but a man . . .' "

"Henry V," Matt said. "I wonder how many good soldiers have been needlessly killed because some psychotic officer took that damn play too seriously. You just wanted the word 'nakedness' in the conversation. Anyway, that doesn't change the fact that—"

"Matt," the president said, slightly annoyed, "shut up and kiss me already."

"Is that an executive order?"

"I kind of hoped I wouldn't need one."

Matt took her face in his hands and found himself reminded in the most pleasant way possible that the president of the United States was a really good kisser. And then she held him in closely, the kind of embrace that happens only once in a relationship; the one in which the ice between two people, both very attracted to each other, is shattered completely in the very first moment of intimacy. And even better, because this time was the second time around.

I can't believe this, Matt thought as he inhaled the sweet aroma of the president's hair. *The leader of the free world is in my arms and trembling like a caged hummingbird. And she's having the same effect on me. Because it's still Ann.*

She looked up at him and smiled. "If you're thinking of me as the president right now, I'm calling in the Secret Service and having you thrown out the window," she whispered.

"Ann," he said, then kissed her again.

The phone shrilled. "Oh, for Christ's sake," she groaned. "Yes," she sighed, hitting the speaker button on the nearest phone.

"Ma'am, you're needed in the sit-room. Something's come up."

Matt kissed her hand and nodded vigorously.

"I'll be right there," she replied, stifling a giggle. She hung up. "Well, so much for our first date."

"Our *second* first date," Matt corrected her. Matt stood up, still holding her hand. "I have to get back anyway. Which reminds me, how do I get back?"

"It's taken care of," she said. "When can I see you again? If you want to—don't feel pressured or anything. I'm serious about that. I mean, if you want to leave it where we left it three years ago . . ."

"Nah, it's just my career," he replied lightly. "Of course I want to see you again. Jesus, Ann, I haven't been with anyone either. Question is, how? And when?"

"We'll think of something. I'll call you later—if you're sure you don't mind."

The little note of insecurity in her voice touched him. They weren't a president and a naval officer, and they never could be. Once again, they were Ann and Matt.

"Of course, call me," he said.

"I'd give you my number," she said, "but then what'd

happen if it didn't work out between us? I'd have to change my number and . . . it'd be a real pain."

She went into his arms. She was a tall woman but he was a taller man, and they fit together perfectly. It was warm, familiar territory. They kissed a final time. "I've gotta go," she whispered. "And I have to fix myself up. It simply wouldn't do to look all debauched as I solve the problems of the free world."

Their hands slid apart. "Good-bye, Ann," he said.

"It better not be, Matt." As she left the room, two Secret Service agents entered. He wondered if they knew what had been going on. Of course they did, they were professionals.

"This way, Captain," one of them said.

"How do I get out of here without being seen?" he asked.

"Not a problem, Captain. We have a car with blacked-out windows to get you to Andrews."

"Thank you, Mr. . . ."

"Hawkins," the agent replied. "Oh, and Captain?"

"Mr. Hawkins."

"You hurt that lady and I'll break your ankles."

"**SO,** who is she?" Jeanne-Marie Fournier asked with a smirk. They were sitting in the crew office having morning coffee. Claude Monroe and Jeanne nodded at each other.

"Captain's got a girl," Claude sang. "Come on, Matt. If you can't tell us, who can you tell?"

"What makes you think there's a girl?" Matt demanded.

"You obviously got no sleep last night."

"I always have trouble sleeping when it gets this close to a mission."

"Yeah, okay, sure," Claude replied.

"Matt?" Jeanne asked with feigned innocence. "Who is Ann?"

Matt blushed. "How the hell do you know her name?"

"Message for you," Jeanne said. " 'Ann's' office called. Will call again at eight. Will call again at eight-thirty. Will call again at nine. Will call again"—the phone chirped—"now, I suppose. Tell 'Ann' I said hello."

Matt picked up the phone. "Yes?"

"Can you talk?"

"Nope."

"Would you like to see me again?"

"Yup."

"This weekend?"

"Yup."

Jeanne and Claude were pointing at him and giggling.

"Camp David? I can have a Gulfstream—"

"Nope."

"What do you mean 'nope'?"

"Not there; it'd be too creepy. We'll talk about it later. Okay?"

"You know, Matthew, one of the things that attracted me to you almost immediately was your scintillating conversational skill." With a chuckle, she rang off.

"Can we get to work now," he said, "or do I have to pull rank?"

"LOOKING good, *Forlorn Hope*, continuing countdown, T minus twenty minutes, seven, six . . ." Commander Ralph Jordan pronounced. He had agreed to delay joining the fleet to serve as capcomm during the launch.

Lying on his back in the front left seat, Matt Wiener looked through his bubble helmet at Jeanne-Marie Fournier, who was scanning the dials in the seat to his right.

"Too hot!" shouted Bob Rodgers from the rearmost seat in the spacecraft.

"We're not redlining anywhere," Matt shouted back. "What the hell is going on?"

Alex Rayne's calm voice cut through. "Abort, *Forlorn Hope*, we're shutting you down now."

"Roger, abort simulation, shutting down," said the cap-comm. "Copy that, *Forlorn Hope*?"

"Son of a bitch!" Matt barked. "Yes, I copy, goddamn it!"

Matt pulled off his helmet and drummed his fingers impatiently while technicians zoomed up the gantry to pry the astronauts through the hatch.

"What was all that about?" Matt demanded of Bob Rodgers when they were safely out of the ship.

Rodgers made a pained "I can't come out and say it" face at Matt.

"Come on, Bob!" Matt said.

"The isolation filters," Rodgers whispered urgently. "They're not strong enough. The . . . things . . . in there . . . it's too dangerous."

"Crew meeting now! In Conference Room A."

Alex Rayne met them at the bottom of the gantry. "Okay, debrief now in the—"

"Later," Matt cut him off. "Crew *only*."

Still in their spacesuits, the crew filed into the conference room. Unlike his predecessor on the *Lifespring*, Matt had no qualms whatsoever about sitting at the head of the table: that was one command perk he had damned well earned.

The crew exchanged looks. They had seen Matt peeved before, but they had never seen him in so cold a fury.

"Lieutenant Rodgers," Matt ordered.

The sudden formality chilled Rodgers. He stood up. "Sir."

"Hand me your launch keys. Now."

"Sir, I can't—"

Matt took a piece of White House stationery from his flap pocket. "Read this."

The paper was passed down the table to Rodgers, who read it and blanched. His brilliant career was now smoke up a chimney. Rodgers pulled the keychain from around his neck and tossed it to Matt.

"Thank you, Bob," Matt replied, suddenly becoming pleasant. "Butch, tell Mr. Rayne he can come in now."

The junior member of the crew went out the door and nodded to Rayne, who was standing just outside.

"There're two choices, Alex," Matt began before Rayne was seated. "Either those nukes are taken off my ship or the isolation area is reinforced, and it's done tonight."

Rayne glared at Bob Rodgers.

"Leave Bob alone," Matt said. "He's protected by someone with a lot more juice than you'll ever have. You get that done. Now."

"Who do you think you're talking to?" Rayne demanded in a low, menacing tone.

"Just get it done, Alex. I'm not risking the lives of this crew—"

"But you'll risk the lives of everyone on this planet instead—"

"We don't know that."

"Oh, really?" Rayne looked at everyone in the room. "Well, I don't know that either. But I'm not taking that chance, and neither are you. I don't care who you've got in your pocket."

"Reinforce that area, Alex. Do it now, or we all walk."

"Oh, is that how it is, Matt? Pulling rank now? I still run this program, no matter what friends you may think you have."

Matt reddened. "What the hell is that supposed to mean?"

"You tell me, Matt. Maybe I'd throw my weight around too *if I were the one boinking the president of the United States!*" As soon as he'd said it, Alex knew he'd gone too far. He even closed his eyes and emitted a pained "ooh."

All that stood between Alex Rayne and a sure trip to the hospital was quick action on the part of Claude Monroe, who jumped up and restrained Matt from leaping across the table at Alex.

Jeanne-Marie Fournier, as much of a gossip addict as the next Parisian, delightedly thought, Oh, *that* Ann. But her voice was icy as she said, "Monsieur Rayne, you are way out of line, sir."

"Why don't you get the hell out of here, Mr. Rayne," Claude Monroe suggested. Rayne, feeling ashamed and chastened, complied quickly.

Claude loosened his grip on Matt and patted him on the shoulder before sitting down. The room was quiet and tense.

"Well," Doralee Conger-Levin said after a long silence, "I guess that shoots the hell out of double dating."

The tension in the room burst and the crew fell about laughing. In truth, the crew were all thrilled at the prospect, like children who had been told that their kind and lovable new stepmother was an heiress, and that they should leave nothing to their imaginations when making out their Christmas lists.

Bob Rodgers was particularly relieved; his career was once again a golden road.

"Just so you know," Matt said, "we've only had one date, and it wasn't even a date, not really. We used to be an item when she was a senator."

"But you are going to see her again," Jeanne prompted him.

"With just a few weeks left? And then I won't see her for a year?"

"If I may, Captain," John Ryham began, "it's very important that our commander be in good spirits during our long journey. I therefore suggest that we pull together on this."

"You mean, grab Matt's slack whenever we can," Claude remarked.

"Uh, exactly. So I suggest we all get to work and give the captain his weekend."

There were murmurs of assent from around the table.

"Uh, one thing, Matt," Butch Caldwell spoke up. "When can we meet her?"

"You've already met her."

"I know we've *met* her," Butch replied. "But we want to *meet* her. You know, not as the president. As the Captain's chick."

"Later," Matt said. "T minus twenty days and counting, children. Let's get back to work."

The idea of going to Camp David for a tryst with the president, even though it was Ann, was simply too strange a prospect for Matt to even contemplate. It would cause a logistical nightmare, but Matt suggested that she come to Houston and spend the weekend in his penthouse. He had to be within shouting distance of the Space Center anyway, and when the weekend was over, the entire crew would be off to Cape Canaveral for final flight preparations and launch.

Having made sure the world and the country were safe, for the moment anyway, President Ann Catesby set about making her own travel arrangements. It was borderline impossible for the president to go anywhere in secret, but over the strenuous objections of the White House Secret Service detail, she gave it her best shot.

The presidential helicopter, *Marine One*, was out of the question for transport to Andrews, since the very cough of its ignition attracted the media like raw meat to a school of piranha, no matter what the hour. Finally, the president took matters into her own hands. She called in Agent Hawkins.

"Irv, who's got the fastest personal car in the detail?"

"That'd be Williams, ma'am. He's got a Mustang Cobra."

"Get him in here."

It was with some slight trepidation that the junior agent in the detail went in for his first private presidential audience.

"How'd you like to help me out, Williams," she said when the agent arrived in her office.

"Anything I can do, ma'am."

"Lend me your car?" Williams looked at his boss in surprise. It was a running joke among the detail that Williams would never allow even his wife to so much as touch his beloved Cobra, much less drive it.

"Ma'am, I can't—" He stopped in horror as he realized what he was almost about to do. "Of course, ma'am," he said, trying not to allow the effort it took to creep into his voice.

"Thank you, Williams. Is it charged?"

"Ready to go, ma'am."

"A Cobra, I understand. I'm a Mustang Sally from way back. Had a GT in college. I do hope it's a stick shift."

"Wouldn't drive anything else, ma'am."

"I miss internal combustion engines, though, filthy as they were. Thank you, Williams. Don't worry, I'll take good care of her. You are insured, aren't you? Just kidding."

A few minutes after one in the morning, with the president behind the wheel and Hawkins sweating and palpitating beside her, the Cobra roared down Pennsylvania Avenue to the Beltway. The president, who missed driving herself and had always loved fast muscle cars, was exhilarated.

"Cheer up, Irv. It'll all be over soon."

"That's what I'm afraid of, ma'am."

The trip took only a few minutes at top speed. The Maryland state police were informed over their own frequency not to even think about pulling over the canary yellow Cobra convertible rocketing down the Beltway toward Andrews, and they arrived at the air base's north gate in record time.

Although any plane the president boarded, whether it was a Boeing 797 or a Piper Cub, automatically became *Air Force One*, the designation was not used on this flight.

She opted for the same Gulfstream that had brought Matt to her several nights before. The flight crew were each asked two simple questions: Do you want to be transferred to the Aleutians? and Who was your passenger tonight? Fortunately for their careers, each answered "No" to the first question and "What passenger?" to the second.

Landing in Houston, the president was whisked into a waiting car and arrived in the garage of Matt Wiener's building in twenty minutes. When Irv Hawkins used his set of digital lockpicks to let her into Matt's apartment, the place was quiet and dark. She quietly walked through the living room into the master bedroom, noting in the ambient light the luxurious appointments with approval, already feeling at home. Matt was asleep, snoring soundly.

She regarded him fondly. "If this relationship is going to go anywhere at all," she said aloud, "we have got to do something about that snoring. It still drives me nuts."

Then she slipped out of her clothes, got into bed, and snuggled up next to him with an arm around his waist. In his sleep, he purred and burrowed his body deeper into hers.

In a few moments, she too was asleep, snoring every bit as soundly.

SIX

THE planet Kivlan, despite Ralph Jordan's gloomy assessment, wasn't really at war. It had just spent the last year in a really crummy mood.

Kivlan's rejection of contact with the *Lifespring* was inconsistent with its character. While Kivlan had no ambitions in space, they would have, under any other circumstances, heartily welcomed visitors. Kivlanians had evolved into a satisfied and accommodating race, living in emotional and ergonomic ease. They had found that saying yes was a lot easier than saying no; yielding the right of way was less taxing than arguing about it; and a smile took far less work than a frown.

All of the twenty-seven nations of Kivlan were prosperous, crime rates were low, and there hadn't been a war in three hundred years. The planet was generous with its natural bounty, and technology had advanced far enough so that no one had to work too hard to exploit it. Yet Kivlan's resources were husbanded rather than pillaged; it was ultimately less work to keep up supplies indefinitely through judicious use than to someday have to go through the trouble of finding alternatives.

The average Kivlanian lived in a one-story dwelling, as climbing stairs was considered a ridiculous waste of energy. Most appliances and conveniences were thought-controlled and self-maintaining. A Kivlanian went home, thought seriously about a *rantta* dinner (pork chops), and in about five minutes, it would be on the table. Then perhaps a *civo* (a movie) or a *rola-civo* (a comedy movie) or a *kana-civo* (a porno movie) before going to sleep in a bed that conformed perfectly to the body of each individual who laid down in it. In the morning, one stepped into a *driska* box and in half an hour the day's fitness workout was complete.

There were cars and motorways and air transports on Kivlan. Cars were run on zero-point energy like everything else on Kivlan, but cars were not actually driven; that would require too much work. Vehicles were programmed according to destination and did all the work while the operator stretched out in a comfortable clublike seat and relaxed. Air travel was the same way; the pilot monitored systems, but that was all.

Kivlanians really didn't have to work too hard at anything, and that was the way they liked it. The emergence of this technology had taken centuries, but now that it was here, everyone did their best to enjoy it.

However, just because no one *had* to work hard didn't mean that no one ever did. There were always those who enjoyed work, and they entered government, the military, medicine, law, and the planet's largest single industry—leisure. Someone had to keep the resorts and theme parks and theaters running up to snuff, and those who did were paid handsomely, and, in keeping with planetary tradition, given very long vacations. All in all, Kivlan was a very agreeable planet on which to reside. Until now.

The four chemical eruptions discovered by the crew of

the *Lifespring* were in fact volcanic in nature, and necessary for the planet's stability—Kivlan was, in the truest sense of the word, blowing off steam. The problem was that the reaction of the fallout that came with the eruptions, combined with the dry winds they caused, made everyone on the planet's surface extraordinarily cranky, not unlike the foehns of the Southern Alps, or the Santa Ana winds in California. Even worse, it caused dry skin and itching and scaling, resulting in the one condition Kivlanians hated most—discomfort.

This was a phenomenon that occurred every seven hundred years or so. However, the last time it had happened, Kivlan was still in its Middle Ages, still backward and superstitious, so the cataclysmic war that had followed was put down to ambitious world leaders and nothing else. And now it was happening again.

The Tranquil Planet was now anything but. Tempers were short and flared often. Wherever there were people, there were altercations—and a great deal of scratching.

The leaders of all Kivlan's twenty-seven nations, and the president of the World Congress, had convened in emergency session at Shileragh Beach in southeastern Vidare to discuss the matter. The choice of an ocean resort was no accident—only in the salt water was there any relief at all. There, all of the leaders of the planet's nations, Kivlan's most distinguished and respected men and women, met with solemn urgency to tackle the problem that was undermining Kivlan's beloved way of life. The sessions lasted hours, but were always suspended at midday for lunch and a swim. Kivlan might have been in trouble, but it was still Kivlan. Even its most courtly and dignified citizens required and demanded leisure time like everyone else. More importantly, the ocean was waiting.

Grig Holma, the president of Vidare, Kivlan's most powerful country, dove and then surfaced, snorting like a bull. He breast-stroked over to a raft and, with much effort, heaved his massive bulk up and over the side, almost upending the raft in the process.

"Hey, watch it, ya big tub o' crap!" shouted an irate Ke Staxa, prime minister of Urno, one of the planet's smaller nations. Fallout itch had struck Staxa particularly hard, and his arms and neck were covered with rashes. This made him even crankier than usual.

"Bite me," Holma grunted, flopping down onto the raft.

"Very mature, very presidential," remarked Eog Roqa, president of Gaius, the planet's second-largest country.

"Why don't you kiss my pucker, Eog," Staxa retorted. "You spend enough time kissing his."

The preceding exchange is an approximate translation. Each leader was speaking his own language. "Kiss my pucker," for example, was actually *"stre ma nogec"* in Urnese. However, multilingual facility was a gift inherent to most Kivlanians, who eased smoothly from one language to another in the general course of conversation.

"Gentlemen, please," said Tapu Pari, the president of the World Congress. "If we can't get along, how can we expect our people to do the same?"

The World Congress was mostly a regulatory body for international commerce; therefore Pari had no real power. He had been invited only to act as a nonvoting parliamentary chairman.

"Get stuffed, Pari," Roqa said. "We're not in chambers now."

"I don't have to take that from you, *srubiw*!"

Srubiw was a fighting word on Kivlan, for which there was no literal or even approximate English translation.

"Oh, you want a piece of me, is that it?"

"I'm hungry," Grig Holma said, ending the argument. "Who wants lunch?"

The mood of tension burst as quickly as it had begun. That was the nature of Kivlan's present affliction; the flareups were only temporary, and faded almost as soon as they appeared. But they appeared often.

"Okay, everybody's sorry, let's have a little self-control here," Pari said.

"Let's have a buffet," Grig Holma suggested. Another raft surfaced from the water, and platters of cold cuts and other delicacies materialized.

"What? No *batcha*?" A giant Kivlanian equivalent of a turkey leg appeared and Holma grabbed it.

"When are you going to tell us about it?" Ke Staxa said accusingly to Grig Holma. "How long are you going to keep it to yourself?"

"What are you talking about?" Holma demanded irritably. He hated being interrupted when he was eating a turkey leg.

"You had visitors, didn't you?" Staxa looked up at the sky to drive home his point.

"Yeah," Pari added. "We live on this planet, too. We have a right to know."

"Can I eat first?" Holma said.

For an answer, Staxa snatched the drumstick out of Holma's greasy paw and chucked it into the water.

"What the hell's wrong with you?" Holma demanded.

Staxa spread his hands as if for affirmation from an invisible audience. "What are we, stupid? We can monitor transmissions from space too, you know."

"Oh, that," Holma said dismissively.

"Yes, that."

"It was nothing. They showed up, and we told them to go home."

"You told them to go home," Staxa said dubiously. "And they did, just like that. They probably traveled billions of miles, took them God knows how long to get here, and they just went home because you asked them to."

Holma shrugged. "Well, we gave them a little encouragement."

"What do you mean, 'a little encouragement'?"

"We gave them a few rounds. Look," Holma continued

over everyone's groans, "we didn't hit them. We just scared them off. It was for their own protection."

"Our first contact, a defining moment in our world's history," Staxa was struggling to remain in control, *"and you shoot at them?"*

"We couldn't receive them now, like this," Holma argued. "I ask you, are we in any condition now to entertain visitors? The Squabbling Planet? They'll think we're a bunch of losers! And quite frankly, right now, that's just what we are."

"Well, tell us *something* about them," Pari said.

"They seemed very nice," Holma said. "Interesting language. Absolutely beautiful music. Kind of a warlike past, but they could be over it now. And *funny* jokes. I mean, real side-splitters. 'These two *qicas* walk into a *sluva*—' "

"Jokes. He's telling jokes. Our planet's going to hell and he's telling jokes. The last time this happened, need I remind you, our planet had a global war. One third of the population was killed off. It took an entire century to recover. What if that happens now? We can kiss our world good-bye!"

"We're not going to war," Holma jeered. "Not unless you really start to piss me off, Staxa."

"Hey, we may be small, but it's all muscle. We could still kick your ass—"

"Stop this!" shouted Tapu Pari. "Do you *hear* what you're saying? Now, stop this nonsense! Shake hands and apologize."

"What is this, a schoolyard?" Holma said wearily.

"He's got turkey grease all over his mitts," Staxa complained.

"What is wrong with you people?" Pari demanded.

"It's a seven-hundred-year virus, pal," Roqa said. "In case you haven't heard. It tends to make people a little edgy."

"Well, I don't care! You are the most brilliant, the best

this planet has to offer. Half of you are the reason why I went into government in the first place. You've helped build this wonderful world of ours. People are going to remember your achievements . . . hundreds . . . thousands of years from now! You are *greatness*. And now, at this moment, you're all acting like a bunch of . . . *assholes!*"

"Hey. Hey, Tapu." Roqa patted his shoulder comfortingly. "It's okay. We can't help it. We don't mean anything by it." Roqa stopped to scratch his neck, a process that involved so much of his concentration that he completely forgot the subject of discussion.

"Well, you're going to have to," Pari replied, weeping in frustration. "Two billion people are depending on you." He shuddered and ran the back of his hand across his eyes.

Staxa looked down, ashamed. "I'll make every possible effort," he said.

"I will if you will," Holma said.

"And what about the visitors?" Roqa asked, whose itch had subsided.

"Oh, they'll be back, I'm sure of it."

"And what do we do?"

"Let's take it one step at a time," Pari said. "We've enough problems with our own people. The extraterrestrials can damned well wait their turn."

GRIG Holma stepped inside the presidential bungalow and kicked the sand from his slippers.

"Ma!" he called.

"In here, dear," his mother replied. Holma padded into the sunroom, where Leva Holma was being exercised in the driska box.

"Did you have a nice swim, dear?"

"Yeah," he called.

"Yes," his mother corrected him.

"Yes," he amended. "But then we . . . aaah, I got into

an argument with Ke Staxa, and then we were carrying
on like a bunch of—"

"You must show more self-control, son," she admonished him, her breathing labored from her exertions. "You
are, after all, the most powerful man in the world. It is
neither dignified nor appropriate behavior."

"Sometimes I can't help it, Ma," he replied shamefacedly. "None of us can."

"That is no excuse. I can help it—why not you?"

"Everybody's different, Ma. Look, you don't even have
the rash. Yech, I feel cruddy."

"You don't get enough exercise," she scolded. "And
when are you going to *get* married?"

"Oh, Ma! Who'd marry me?"

"The president of Vidare? Why, I should think, just
about anyone."

"Ma, I'm fat. I'm a slob. I'm about as interesting to
look at as a plate of *zingla*."

"You're also the most brilliant man in Vidare. Let's not
hear any more of that sort of talk." She stepped out of the
driska box and toweled her face.

"Now listen to me, son. You must save our planet from
itself. To do that, you must be relaxed. To be relaxed, you
need a wife."

"Ma, I know you want grandchildren—"

"Yes, I do, but that's not a pressing concern at the
moment. You have certain needs—"

"Ma-aa!" Holma blushed.

"You're ninety-six years old, Grig. How much longer
do you want to wait? Who's going to take care of you? I
won't be here forever."

"Oh, Mother, you'll outlive us all. First things first,
Ma." He thought of a *salika*, a triple-decker sandwich,
and it appeared before him.

"In the driska box before you take a bite," his mother
warned him.

"Aw, Ma!"

"You told me you just had lunch."

Like a reluctant schoolboy ordered to finish his chores before playing ball, Holma clumped his way into the box. Even though the driska did all the work, Holma still hated it.

"Now," his mother began, "you were saying."

"You're an engineer, Ma," Holma said. "I've been working on a theory, and I need your opinion, your technical know-how."

"All right, son. Go ahead."

"I think we've been looking at this problem in the wrong way. We've been thinking it's chemical—the reaction of the fallout with our brain chemistry."

"Continue."

"But," he said, beginning to breathe heavily as the driska's intensity increased, "if that's the case, why haven't we found a drug that works to counteract it?"

"Maybe such a drug doesn't exist," she replied.

"No, it should exist. We know the chemical makeup of the fallout, and we know the chemical makeup of our own bodies. Therefore, we should have found the right interaction by now."

"That makes sense," she replied approvingly. Such a genius, her son. Why hadn't some bright, charming woman snapped him up long ago?

"So what I was thinking, Ma, is maybe it's not chemical at all. I mean, I know I'm not a scientist, but it makes sense, doesn't it?"

"Then, logically, what would your solution be?"

"I might be way off base here, Ma, but I was thinking . . . electrical."

"Hmm! Interesting. Why would you say electrical?"

"Correct me if I'm wrong. The Kivlanian body is made up of a whole bunch—okay, I don't know how much. I'm a historian, and I just remember hearing it somewhere, but we've got electricity in our bodies, right? Enough to run a transport for a week, or something like that?"

Leva Holma shrugged, but was proud of the way her son's mind worked. "Something like that. Though we've never found much use for electricity here on Kivlan. But do go on."

"Okay, okay; what if the fallout is somehow reacting negatively to the electricity in our bodies—not the chemistry?"

"It's a thought. But how?"

"Ma! How should I know? It's a theory." He looked at his mother in anticipation. "Well, what do you think?"

"I think it's brilliant. Even if you're wrong, the theory has merit." She went over to the driska box and smoothed her son's hair from his eyes. "So handsome," she said.

"A face only a mother could love," Holma replied.

"What else is bothering you, son?"

"Isn't that enough?"

She gave him her standard mom look, from which he knew he could never hide.

"It's these Earth people, Ma."

"Oh, them," she replied dismissively. "Didn't you say, after studying the package they sent you, that they were about a thousand years behind us, technologically, socially, anthro—"

"Yes, I did. And now, I've changed my mind."

As usual, his mother didn't argue with him, preferring instead to know the workings of his mind.

"Look, Ma, we—" He shifted in discomfort. "Can't I get out of this damn box?"

"Language! And no, ten more minutes. Go on."

"Okay, based on what we've learned, yes, they're behind us, way behind us, as far as the way they live everyday life. But that's minor. Who cares if they have to cook their own food or drive their own cars, clean their own houses? Trivialities! They've got the technology to get *here*, don't they?"

"What is it, son?" she asked with concern.

"Mommy, I don't understand these people! They're either crazy or—they *are* crazy!"

"*Sshhh*, calm down. Tell me."

"They have this music, this unbelievably beautiful music, I swear, it gave me chills! They have this writer, he wrote things like 'We are such stuff as dreams are made on.' " That's just one line—the fellow wrote thousands of gems like that! He must have been a god! Oh, this other guy, he sang songs—how did he do it! There's one line, I guess it's a love song, maybe it lost something in the translation, but it's something like 'you are the promised kiss of springtime that makes the lonely winter seem bright . . .' Why, it never even occurred to anyone on Kivlan to write words like that!"

Leva Holma was visibly moved. "They sound like a charming race of people," she said. "They sound wonderful."

"Well, yes, but Ma! I read their history. Death! Murder! Wars!"

"We've had wars, Grig."

"Not like this, Mom. Only a hundred, no, less, less than a hundred of their years ago, that's practically *yesterday*, they had this . . . this maniac! Because of him, there was a war that killed fifty million people! Fifty *million*! That's almost half the entire population of Vidarc! There was another guy, *at the same time*—he killed millions of his own people, even before the war started! Murdered them—*starved* them to death! It's all over the place! And they've had religious wars—over the centuries, millions of people murdered because they didn't believe what others believed. Ma, I don't get it! How can a race of people be capable of such beauty . . . *and* such brutality?"

Leva Holma looked at her son with affection. What a fine, decent man he had become. How fortunate for Vidare that it was presided over by a man with such feeling. And how she ached for him.

"Son," she began, "there is little I can say that can help

you. You know better than I of the sadder chapters of our own history. But I think, from what you've told me, that these people are trying. I think they *are* self-aware. Why else would they want to come here in peace? Why would they show us *both* their beauty *and* their horror? They've hidden nothing, Grig. I think that's admirable."

"You do?" he asked doubtfully.

"I do. What if they gave you their music and their poetry, and nothing else? And then, only later, you discovered their murderous past? These are a fine people, Grig. Primitive, perhaps. Flawed, definitely. But they want to learn. They want to evolve. Give them a chance, Grig."

"If that's true, Mother, then I cannot allow them on this planet just yet."

"Why not?"

"Because unless we fix our own problem here, first, who knows what will happen when they return? Mother, I *fired* at them, just to frighten them away for their own good, but they'll be back. They're a curious people, I can feel it. And this time, they'll be ready. Who knows what will happen?" he repeated.

"Then you'd better get busy," his mother told him.

"Yes, I should. *Now* can I get out of this stupid thing, Mom?"

"By all means. And by the way, I'd like a look at their information package. I'd like to learn some of their language and customs. I want to be ready for their next visit."

SEVEN

TALUNA Merz was damned tired. That was no rare condition. Merz was always tired. He was weary when he arose in the morning, fatigued at work, and exhausted by the time he got home at night. Even the driska box failed to invigorate him. He knew why, too. His life had fallen apart. His wife of twelve years had left him; he had reached a dead end in his job as a city engineer for Darais, a winter resort town on the northwestern coast of Vidare; and his ten-year-old car had given up the ghost, forcing him to rely on public transport, which added an hour each way to his daily commute. On top of all that, the fallout rash was driving him bonkers.

No longer expecting the miracle of happiness in his life ever again, all Taluna asked for was a cold one at the end of the day. That was all: no romance, no wealth, no dreams-come-true—just a nice cold beer with a snowy one-inch head of foam and cool moisture dripping down the sides of the glass. Vidarean beer was the best on Kivlan, and in Darais it was the best of all. It was pretty much the last pleasure Taluna had in life, and it had become the high point of his day.

Like most homes in Darais, Taluna's was constructed of an adobelike brick, one story with a vestigial turret on each side. The inside was quite bare, as a benumbed Taluna had stood motionless and wordless as his wife had systematically removed everything but the bed and a small table and chair. His home, which had once been warm and welcoming, was now bare and cold . . . like the inside of my soul, Taluna thought melodramatically. He tried to laugh it off; his wife had met someone else, and he had been lucky that they had stayed together as long as they did. He'd never again find someone who jolted his heart as she had. And even if he did, with his luck, she'd probably have a boyfriend. But his gallant attempt to find humor in the situation rang hollow.

It was at the end of another predictably empty day when he sprawled on the floor as usual and thought of a cool, dark Daraisian Special. In a moment, his hand was filled with a foaming beaker. He brought it to his lips and drank deeply and gratefully.

And his throat caught fire.

He stared at the glass in horror. It looked like a Special, it tasted somewhat like a Special, but—

The fire was spreading to his stomach.

"MedCentral!" he shouted.

"MedCentral," a pleasant, preprogrammed voice responded. *"List symptoms . . . now. Thank you."*

"I ordered a beer, but it's not a beer! My throat!" he gagged. "My stomach . . ."

"Remain motionless for light sensor. Thank you." A needle point of light traced a line from his head to his toes.

"Stand by for findings. Thank you. Diagnosis: ingestion of sendithylate. Prognosis: terminal. Thank you."

"What the hell do you mean, terminal?" he gasped.

"E.T.A. of meditrans: two minutes five seconds. Your

expiration: twenty-six point eight seconds. Thank you."

"I'm dying? But I only wanted a beer!"

"Remain motionless for light sensor. Thank you."

"What the hell for, you prerecorded bitch!"

The light sensor reappeared.

"No ingestion of beer evident. Thank you. And don't call me a bitch. Butthole. Thank you."

"I always thought . . . I'd go . . . like a hero . . . or with my . . . family . . . around me . . . this is so . . . ludicrous . . . it figures . . ."

"Sir. Please respond. Respond. Respond. Remain motionless for light sensor. Thank you. MedCentral extends its condolences on your recent demise. Coroner recovery team has been dispatched, E.T.A.: five point seven minutes. Thank you. Division of Probate has been alerted. Thank you. Have a nice day. And thank you for calling MedCentral."

RANO Pedru's day wasn't as awful as that of Taluna Merz, but it came close. The premiere *civo* (film) director in Gaius, he was fond of saying, "What the hell, even *I* come up with a dog once in a while." His current movie in production was definitely shaping up to be one of the canine variety. The actors were sleepwalking, the crew was uninspired, and the script, which had read so beautifully, was not translating onto film with the dash that it had promised. Everyone was losing interest fast.

"All right, everybody shut up!" he shouted. He concentrated and thought "lights." Normally, a loud bell would then sound and get everyone quiet and in place as the lights automatically set to the desired intensity, and the sound recorder would achieve speed immediately. In this case, however, nothing happened. Again he thought "lights." Again nothing happened. Finally, with the clock running and money ticking away, he lost his temper. "Let's go lights!" he shouted. "I said, lights! Hey, jerk-weed!" he yelled in the general direction of the thought processor, "I said, *lights!*"

The explosion was deafening.

Every light and every camera had burst into flame. Fortunately, no one was seriously injured, one of those rare, foolishly lucky occasions where the blast channeled upward instead of outward.

Rano Pedru was knocked off his feet, but came to immediately, dazed and unsteady.

"Print it," he rasped. "Lunch, one hour."

THE Crevan War Games, a joint exercise held annually by participating members of the world's navies, was the highlight of the year's training schedule. Despite the fact that the planet had been at peace for several hundred years, no one seriously believed that the world was yet safe enough to dispense with national security. Each country had well-trained and well-equipped defense forces, and all adhered to the philosophy that the only lasting peace was peace through strength.

Generation upon generation of soldiers, sailors, and air crew had served entire careers without ever having heard a shot fired in anger, yet few in the military believed that their constant and intensive training had gone to waste. The primary mission of the defense forces was to prevent war and also, although this was never said aloud, to guarantee the continuity of a significant part of each nation's economy. Just as on Earth, the military provided employment, not only in its ranks but to a host of peripheral industries as well.

The military was also a world unto itself, with proud traditions and a profound code of honor. As on Earth, those who served considered themselves a breed apart, far above the banal existence of those who did anything else. Any soldier could have remained a *craduwa griet* (lizard-shit civilian) and become a success in any field of endeavor; but it took grit to leave all that behind to serve one's country.

The Crevan War Games were the ultimate reward for the year's hard work. They were extremely expensive, and most nations could only afford to participate once every few years. Only Vidarc and Gaius had the budgets to allow attendance on an annual basis.

The two nations, although fast friends, were foes each year at the games. Each headed an alliance that included one or more other nations. The purpose of the maneuvers was to pit two massive armadas against each other, with the express purpose of destroying the opposing fleet and landing an invasion force at the enemy capital.

Of course, no real shots were fired and no invasion force was landed anywhere. It was like any other war game, with referees informing ships that they had been sunk and were out of the maneuver. The first flagship to sight the enemy coast with at least ten surviving troop transports was declared the winner.

In reality, however, everyone was the winner. All the participants loved the challenge, but it was the partying that went on after the maneuvers were concluded that were the real fun. Every single member of every fleet was invited to attend, and few from any nation ever missed it.

The tiny principality of Creves had no Navy of its own, only a Coast Guard. But it did have entertainment like nowhere else on Kivlan. It was the equivalent of Atlantic City, the Côte d'Azur, and Disney World all rolled into one. Everyone in Creves benefited from the games, as the small nation became as crowded as Palm Springs or Fort Lauderdale during spring break—and equally raucous. But it was all in fun and there was seldom any real trouble. Already rich from tourism, the postmaneuver celebrations infused so much money into its coffers that many of its citizens only had to work the week of the War Games to earn enough for the year. The citizens, therefore, looked forward to the post-games celebrations as much as the participating navies. And this year, the citizens firmly believed, would be the best ever.

And it would have been. Except for one thing.

It didn't happen during the maneuvers, which went off without any problems. Vidare, teamed up with Urno and Lepang, faced off against Gaius, Ruud, and Velax. The Vidarean Alliance had slightly more firepower, but the Gaiusian-led forces had an ace in the hole—a young, newly promoted Velaxian admiral who was the most brilliant strategist any of them had ever seen. The young admiral drew in the enemy with a feint at the opposing armada's center and then a night reversal of fleet order, somewhat reminiscent of Spruance's master stroke at Midway. Having pulled the enemy in, the admiral encircled the opposing fleet, enabling her armada to "cross the T" of many of the Vidarean ships—a maneuver that on Kivlan as well as on Earth spelled victory. The Gaiusian Alliance ships then surged past the remaining ships on both sides, leaving them off balance and hopelessly far behind. The entire Gaiusian Fleet sailed unmolested toward Daribi Bay, in full sight of the Vidarean capital.

The quick-wittedness of the Velaxian admiral was deeply appreciated on both sides, not only for her tactical brilliance but for the early conclusion of the games, which would allow the fun in Creves to begin that much sooner.

The celebrations began with four separate dinners: a gigantic barbecue for the lower ranks, a similar outing for the senior NCOs, a more refined meal for the junior and field-grade officers, and a grand and luxurious feast for the senior command staffs—all of whom wished they were partying in the more relaxed manner of the lower ranks. At those dinners, medals, commendations, and the coveted victory ensigns were presented. After that, the entire complement of all navies was turned loose on the attractions that Creves had to offer.

The brawling began almost immediately.

Although the Crevan celebrations were high-spirited affairs, altercations between or within navies were strictly forbidden. It was considered bad form for the victorious navy to brag or lord it over the vanquished. In fact, it had become a tradition for the victors to buy a round in good fellowship for any of the losers they happened to encounter in the course of their revels. The government of Creves, while they welcomed their guests most heartily, also cautioned them about certain types of behavior that were strictly proscribed, and that included anything that resulted in either physical injury or property damage. In the past, all of the celebrants were able to adhere to these rules without inhibiting their enjoyment. In fact, former enemies normally wound up partying together, exchanging parts of uniforms and forging lasting friendships.

That was then. This was now.

It was later determined that the flashpoint was when a young Velaxian petty officer gave a loud and tactless toast to his admiral. This was taken amiss by a table of Vidarean sailors, who refused to raise their glasses, as they considered the toast bad form. A group of Gaiusians and Ruudians accused them of poor sportsmanship, and an argument ensued, which quickly degenerated into blows. The fight spilled out onto the street, where some sailors tried to put a stop to it, but were drawn into the fight instead. The Shore Patrol was called immediately, supported by Crevan local police, whose numbers were too small to quell the disturbance. The former combatants were still fighting each other, but there still remained a glimmer of fellowship, so all joined together against the authorities. The fight spread quickly and soon enveloped the entire, tightly contained celebration area.

Reinforcements were called in, but it wasn't until the Crevan Army, including its small but elite airborne contingent, arrived on the scene that the disturbance, now a full-fledged riot, was finally put down.

Neither the Crevans nor the combined military authorities could arrest everyone, so in the end, they arrested no one. All of the warring parties were appropriately sheepish about the whole episode, and not a little confused as to how it started or why it got so out of hand.

It was the principality of Creves that ended up in the least enviable position. Their capital city was a shambles, and now so was their economy. The navies had to be fined enough to repair the damage and make up for lost income, but at the same time, Creves did not want such lucrative yearly business to relocate. It was a tough dilemma and there seemed no way out of it.

All of the navies departed in the cold light of the following day, leaving behind them a forlorn wreck of a city. Crevans stood on the docks watching them go, feeling dazed and helpless as their livelihoods sailed away with the fleets. In the middle of the crowd was the Crevan governor-general. He offered up a small prayer to a deity of which he had never in his life asked a thing.

"Help us find a way out of this," he prayed silently. "Don't let my people descend into the hell of poverty. Find us the way!"

THE most celebrated naval officer on all of Kivlan was Ro Heelvar, the vice admiral of the Gaiusian Grand Fleet. He had matured gracefully and seamlessly from being a bright junior officer into a distinguished senior officer. He had excelled in every duty to which he had ever been assigned, whether it was hazardous sea duty or selling the year's defense budget to the legislature.

He was a man of great personal charm and charisma, popular with the lower deck and equally respected in the most rarified circles. In a few more years, he would succeed to the top office in the Gaiusian Navy, admiral of the fleet. He was at the height of his career and his power, at the time in his life when a man can look around him with satisfaction and say, "I've done it. Everything to which I have ever aspired; I have done it all."

Ro Heelvar was the most respected, most admired, and most trusted military officer on the planet. And he was beginning, ever so slowly, to go insane.

There were just over two billion people on Kivlan. Since the eruptions had begun, most of them had reported brief incidents of unprovoked irritability. An estimated ten percent had some form of fallout rash. Of that ten percent, five percent reported brief, violent changes in temperament. Within that five percent were one-half of a percent whose mood swings had become more or less regular, and a minuscule number who had become delusional, as the atom-sized bits of electricity from the fallout met atom-sized bits of electricity in the victim's brain, altering the brain's chemistry in the most subtle of ways. Most of them were in positions where the harm they could render to themselves or to others was minimal. But one of them, unfortunately, was the second highest ranking admiral in the second most powerful navy in the world.

It had started out quite subtly. Heelvar was up late, going over fleet dispositions. He felt his left eyebrow slowly raise, in just the way it had as a small child when he received news of a beloved grandfather's death. The trick was, the eyebrow never really rose; he had even checked in the mirror. It just *felt* that way —and very real, nonetheless. The imagined raising of that left eyebrow was a prelude to a great sadness that would always be followed by tears. It was an emotion, like all of the emotions of the great man, that he had learned to control.

Therefore, many years later, when he felt the ancient but very real sensation of the onset of the sadness of loss come virtually without warning, he had burst into tears, for the first time since childhood. Although he was alone in his grand sanctum of an office, he had still looked about him for a witness to this embarrassing scene. Finding none, he returned his thoughts to his unprecedented outburst and had puzzled on it for hours. Finding no reason for it, he then went on to find out something else: what could be done to prevent it?

"When you are sad," his beloved grandfather, a former Admiral of the Fleet whom he had revered, had told him, "and it seems that nothing in the world will ever cheer you up again—do for others. You'll see. It *will* help."

And it always had. But what could he do now? How could he help others? Kivlan was a peaceful, civilized planet that had abolished the need for wars, but they still had their share of evil people, cruel people, desperate people . . . and those they victimized.

Those poor victims, he thought, the ones who suffer pain—I must help them. I must find a way so that no one ever suffers again . . . and the invisible eyebrow slowly began to elevate.

I must find a way. *I* must. There's no one else in the world who understands. No one else who can save . . . unless. *Unless.* Unless I ran the world. Unless *I* ran Kivlan? Yes, of course, *of course*. But only for good. To help people, to take away their pain. But how would I go about it?

As a senior military officer, Heelvar had access to the highest levels of security. This meant that he was on the replication list, which gave him exact duplicates of everything the Earth ship had sent in its information package. As with everyone who had studied the package, Heelvar was fascinated by its contents. His keen mind immediately picked up on a striking enigma: How could a people so far behind Kivlan in technology and socialization be so far ahead in music and culture? The musical giants they had sent—Mozart, Beethoven, and Sinatra—why, this music was years ahead of their own! And their culture! This Shakespeare—his eyebrow had risen and he had almost wept when he ran the play *Hamlet* through his translator. No one on Kivlan had ever written stories like these!

And yet, what was their history? Nothing but brutality, depravity, and avarice; nothing but long periods of ignorance and war punctuated by brief needlepoints of enlightenment. This planet, unlike Kivlan, had never gone anywhere near three hundred *days* without a war somewhere on its surface, much less three hundred years. It had never, not even *once*, enjoyed a period where peaceful coexistence was total.

It shouldn't surprise me, thought Heelvar. There is a duality in all mankind. Wasn't Kivlan's own history full of maniacs who murdered thousands, yet at the end of the day took their deeply loved children on their knees and sung them sweet lullabies?

Maybe now, at this time in their history, they had finally begun to evolve into a peaceful planet that had left war behind, but Heelvar doubted it. This was a false dawn; Kivlan had had many of them. And they had been fired upon when they tried to approach Kivlan. A stupid if disguisedly well-intentioned action, one that was bound to backfire. Heelvar wondered if he could use this to his advantage. He didn't know what use he could make of the situation if these foreigners returned, *when* they returned. But he knew that he was a fool if he didn't exploit the situation.

For Heelvar knew now that even though his high office gave him a great deal of power, for the first time in his life, and for the good of everyone, he wanted *all* of the power. And perhaps these foreigners could help him achieve it.

He would watch. And wait. And then, when the time was right and the vision became clear . . . he would *act*.

AS it happened, there were bagpipes on Kivlan. The planet also had pianos and violins, but sadly no trumpets or saxophones. There was also some of the digital-alternative-New-Age synthetic music that one raised on sci-fi movies might expect from another planet, but the cold fact was that most people on Kivlan hated it. Synthetic replication might be fine for everyday conveniences, but Kivlanians wanted their music to be natural.

The bagpipe was the one instrument, the single musical sound, that citizens of all nations on Kivlan had in common, much like the bugle on Earth had been the universal call to arms. The lonely, plaintive strains of the bagpipe were held in deep awe and respect throughout Kivlan, as the history of each nation—particularly in war, and later, at war's end and the dawning of an age of peace—was scored by its simple haunting notes.

That was why the bagpipe channel had burst clear and strong amid every other radio signal. If the day's stresses and strains became too oppressive, the piper channel was there to soothe the nerves.

President Grig Holma had been a piper since his early youth. In fact, he had won competitions in college. And every day, when the duties of his office began to crowd him, he would take a half-hour, kick everyone out of his office, break out the pipes, and let it rip. At first it was a joke among his staffers, but his virtuosity soon shut everyone up. He never allowed anyone to stay to hear him, but staffers often momentarily stopped in the middle of their duties and listened outside the door.

Playing helped him to think. He could clear his mind and focus, and then, feeling refreshed, he was ready to tackle problems anew.

The Creves situation was giving him a headache. Honor had to be satisfied and so the fleets had to be punished, but not so much so that they would begin to blame Creves and never hold their celebrations there ever again. Creves had been forced into the uneasy position of a merchant who nabs the child of his best customers for shoplifting; the child should be punished, but at the same time, the merchant doesn't want to embarrass the parents and lose their trade.

It took forty-five minutes of solid piping to come up with the solution. He was putting his bagpipes away when Vice President Dara Widh knocked on his office door and entered. In Vidare, the vice president did not chair the legislature but instead served as the president's chief of staff.

"Mr. President," she greeted him.

"The hell are ya, D?" The two had been close friends since the beginning of their political careers.

She threw herself onto the chaise longue that had served the last twelve presidents—in various capacities. "Grig, I can't tell you how glad I am that you're back!"

"Didn't you like being president for a few days?" he asked with a grin.

She rolled her eyes. "You don't want to know what I think. We have got a serious problem—"

"Fine," he interrupted, "but first things first. The Creves deal."

"This is more important."

"It won't take long. Get the bean counters together. Have them figure out exactly how many sailors and officers of each pay grade—taking into account the corresponding currency differentials for each nation—how much they earn, how much they were going to spend in Creves. Assess from each member of each fleet, from the admirals down to seaman recruits, two thirds of that figure, and pay it directly into an emergency account—like a disaster relief fund—and we'll hand it all over to the Crevans and let them work it out with their people."

The vice president nodded approvingly. "That sounds fair. The sailors know they deserve it, it gets them off the hook, Creves doesn't go broke, and it keeps the door open for next year."

"Common sense," he shrugged. "What's your problem?"

"You're not going to like this, not one bit."

"Well, when you put it that way—"

Dara Widh closed her eyes and took a deep breath. "We have to shut down the thought processors," she said in a rush.

"What?" Grig replied after a long pause.

"I'm sorry, but we have no choice."

"Did you hear what you just said?"

"Yes, I did," she replied softly.

"No. Did you *hear* what you just said?"

"There is no choice, Mr. President."

"D, are you crazy? Have you totally looped the loop? Have you even thought of the repercussions of such an act? I'm not talking about having to make your own sandwiches here, or cleaning your own rug or any of that. Can you imagine the bloodbath on our motorways when people try to drive their own cars? Our aircraft falling out of the sky? Our ships slamming into docks at thirty knots?"

"Grig, the processors aren't working! A fellow in Darais ordered a beer yesterday, and now he's dead! Because the processor didn't give him a beer, it gave him a glass of sendithylate! Things are starting to happen that frighten me! A movie set in Gaius blew up because the director wanted lights! So far the motorways haven't had any bloodbaths, but that can change at any time. Okay, those are just a few things, but can you see where this is going?"

"All right," he said placatingly. He shut his eyes and rubbed his temples. "First things first. Have you called in the minister of science?"

"Yes. Minister Dacos should be outside right now."

"Send him in. I want to know just where we are and just where we're headed."

The vice president had never met the minister of science before. He was a midterm replacement who had been plucked from a research chair at Sgara Fo, one of Vidare's finest universities. She was looking forward to meeting him; he was reputed to be far and away the most brilliant man who had ever been selected for the post.

Dara went out into the president's waiting room to find the minister, but no one was there. She was about to go back into the president's office, when a superbly dressed, somewhat rakish-looking man entered from the bathroom.

"Excuse me," she asked him, "have you seen the minister of sci—"

"Oops, sorry," he said. "Almost missed you. Had to go shake hands with the unemployed. But whoa! If I'd've known it was you, Vice President . . ."

"You're—"

"Hey, I'm a little surprised myself." He extended his hand. "It's okay, I always wash my hands afterwards."

"*You're*—"

"Ted Dacos, Vice President. Pleased to meet you."

"*Ted*? Your name is *Ted*? What kind of name is *Ted*?"

"I know, weird, right? It's my initials, Trazor Eut Dacos. But none of that's important right now. What do you say we get out of here, have a couple drinks, maybe a light supper, go dancing at the Gin-cha, and watch the sun come up tomorrow? I've got a view from my balcony—"

"Minister! Are you forgetting yourself?"

"Never," he chuckled. "What, vice presidents don't eat? They don't watch the sunrise? And call me Ted."

Dara glared in disbelief. "You must get slapped . . . a lot."

He gave her a modest grin that she almost found charming, much to her annoyance. "A lot less than you'd think. A lot less than *I'd* think. Anyway, Vice President, Dara— is it all right if I call you Dara?"

"It is *not*."

"Dara," he began, putting his hand to his heart, "refuse me if you must. But promise me it's only because it's me. I'd hate to see the guy who deserves you, who's right for you, who could make you thrilled to wake up in the morning, lose out because your heart's not open to *anyone*."

"Are you like this with *every* woman you meet?"

"Every woman who makes me feel this way."

"And how many is that?"

"Every woman I meet. But I really mean it this time."

"The president is waiting." She opened the door and motioned him inside. She met the president's eye and shot him a where-did-you-find-this-schmuck glare. Grig tried very hard not to break into laughter but was only moderately successful.

"Good to see you, Mr. President."

"Ted, how are you? Sit down."

"Thank you, sir."

"D, don't let this guy fool you; I didn't appoint him for no good reason. He's one of the most brilliant scientists in Vidare."

"*The* most brilliant."

"And the most modest. You graduated from university at what, six and a half years old?"

"Six years, five months, and twenty-two days, but who keeps track of such things?"

"You said . . . scientist," Dara remarked. "That's a rather generic term, isn't it? Do you have a specialty?"

The minister of science arched his eyebrows.

"I mean . . . in *science*."

"Oh. Well, I've got my doctorate in geology."

"So, you're a geologist, then."

"And physics."

"Oh, so you have—"

"And biochemistry. And astronomy. And medicine. And mathematics. And—"

"Shut up, Ted," the president laughed, "and stop showing off."

"Sorry, sir; it's my nature."

"All right, Ted—sit down and get comfortable, and then give me the bad news. All of it."

"I'd rather stand and walk around. It helps me think. Mr. President, Madame Vice President, I have some good news. Unfortunately, I also have bad news."

"Good news first," Grig said, "I'm feeling nostalgic."

"Sir, the good news is, the eruptions have almost run their course. Another thirty days, forty tops, this whole nightmare will be a memory."

"Why, that's wonderful!" Dara cried. Her hand went involuntarily to the rash on her neck.

"And the bad news," Grig asked.

"The bad news is, it's going to get worse before it gets better."

"I was afraid of that," the president said.

"How can it get worse?" Dara asked. "You said it's almost run its course."

"Think of it this way, Madame Vice President," Ted replied, all traces of flirtation gone from his manner, "think of a container of highly flammable liquid. Expose it to flame, and it'll go up. But not nearly as fast or with the same violent intensity as that container once it is empty of the liquid and only the vapors remain. That's what we're dealing with."

"Are you saying," Dara began, "that our planet is going to *explode*?"

"Absolutely not," he replied firmly. "That was never a danger. However, the fallout that is causing all of our problems will be more intense. Mr. President, you were right, and I don't know how you thought of it because, well, I didn't think of it first. It is our own electrical impulses, when they interact with the fallout, that are causing the problems. In some strange way, they are affecting the way our thought signals are interpreted by the processors."

"I told you!" Dara said triumphantly. "We do have to shut them down!"

"Shut them down and do what?" Grig demanded.

Ted Dacos, who had been thinking furiously, had an idea. "Sir, it might be possible to reconfigure the processors for voice actuation."

"Voice actuation?"

"Sure. Instead of thinking about, say, hamburger, you just say, 'I want a hamburger.' "

"Thank you, Ted. It might have taken me days to figure that out. I know what voice actuation is, thank you. What I meant was, it's a technology that's hundreds of years old. And it never worked all that great to begin with. Why? Because there are over seventy-five languages on this planet. And there are words that mean different things in different languages—not to mention the ones in the same language that mean different things. And people talk funny. They don't pronounce things the same way. Their accents, tone, inflections. Thoughts, on the other hand—mental images, if you will—are universal."

"That's quite true, Mr. President, but unfortunately we have no choice. Who on this planet remembers how to cook? To drive? To mow their own lawn? Can you imagine the overload on MedCentral alone?"

"We can't have that," Grig Holma replied. The president couldn't bear to see people hurt. It was a key aspect of his persona that made him beloved by his people. "How long will it take to reconfigure the processors?"

"One day, sir. If we get the cooperation of the other nations of the world. I promise you, no more than that."

"I'll handle the other nations. The two of you get to work on the reconfiguration."

Dara looked at him in horror. The idea of spending twenty-four hours with Ted Dacos . . . "Mr. President!"

"Just get to work," he snapped, with uncharacteristic stiffness.

"Sir, how are you going to handle the next twenty-four hours?"

"As it happens, I have an idea."

"MY fellow Kivlanians," Grig began, "I speak to you tonight on behalf of all twenty-seven nations, of this, the most beautiful and bounteous planet that has ever been created.

"My friends, I will not lie to you. Our planet is facing its biggest crisis in seven hundred years. The fallout is beginning to affect our everyday lives. And that, fellow Kivlanians, is something we must unite against. I am assured that this condition will last only another four-to-six weeks—but in that time, we must make certain sacrifices that will ensure our well-being until the crisis is over.

"We are therefore going to reconfigure our global thought processors to voice actuation. This will take time—I am told, twenty-four hours. Beginning midnight tonight, and lasting until midnight tomorrow, the processors will be totally off-line. Now, I'm sure you are all aware of the difficulty and inconvenience and, let's face it, the danger this condition might cause. Therefore, I would like all of you to contribute in this way: We are declaring tomorrow Global Feast Day. In other words, everybody gets the day off tomorrow. Tonight, set aside enough food and drink for a full day. MedCentral has been notified and is prepared. Do not touch any comestibles or drink until they have been analyzed.

"By midnight tomorrow, the conversion should be complete. We will keep you abreast of our progress. In the meantime, consider tomorrow a gift. Spend the time at home, with your loved ones. Go to the park, the shore, the lake, or your own backyard."

"I don't know about you, but I've always been annoyed by people who look at a tragedy, or even an inconvenience, and say, 'Oh, but look, some good came out of it.' Well, I was wrong. There is good. Because out of this, we have one extra day to spend with those we love. To create memories we never would have had if tomorrow were just another working day. Who knows? You might walk down the street and find the love of your life. You might be there when your child takes her first step or speaks his first words. You just might discover something about a parent or a spouse that you never had time to notice before. It could happen, and it will happen to someone. And if it doesn't happen to you, at least you will have received one extra day in your life where nothing whatsoever is expected from you except to notice the beauty around you."

"Good night, my dear friends. May Providence bless you, and continue to bless our own wonderful world."

"You son of a bitch," the vice president sniffed, wiping away a tear. "I haven't cried since I was four."

"You know why I was able to do that?" Grig asked her.

"No. Why?" she replied, fighting back another sob.

"Because I meant it. Every single word. Now the two of you—get out of here and get to work."

"What are you going to do?"

"None of your business. Now beat it. Scram. Get lost. You have work to do."

"Yes, sir." Dara and Ted hurried out of the office.

"Wait," Ted halted her as they shut the door behind them.

"Wait for what?"

Ted stuck his ear to the door. When he came away, he was smiling to himself.

In another moment, the strains of the bagpipe came clearly through the door.

TED Dacos had not been exaggerating about his apartment. It occupied the entire 137th floor of a gleaming monolith, with a balcony that went all the way around. The Vidarean sunset seemed close enough to touch.

But Ted was all business as they began to coordinate the reconfiguration efforts from the terminal on his desk.

"Okay, Lepang control, you are configured," he said briskly. "Cleared to test voice actuation. Let me know how it goes before you make it operational."

"Thank you, Minister Dacos, this is Lepang control, we'll keep you informed. Lepang out."

"Okay," he said, yawning and stretching. "Next victim."

"That'll be Velax," Dara replied, consulting her own terminal.

"Thank you, Vice Prez. Hello, Velax control, this is Minister Dacos. How are you on this almost unbearably lovely night?"

"Good evening, Minister, Velax control, can you wait five? The prime minister wants to effect reconfiguration personally."

"That'll be fine, Velax, we need a break anyway. Take your time."

"Thank you, Minister. Velax control out."

Ted leaned back and rotated his left arm. "Aaah! I always get a knot right there, right under my shoulder blade."

For reasons that entirely eluded her, the vice president got up and stood behind the minister of science and began massaging his shoulders.

"Oooh, Providence, that feels good . . . better than sex. Well, not really, but it's right up there."

"Can I ask you a question?" Dara inquired.

"Ask away. Just don't stop."

Dara felt a huge knot beneath his shoulder blade and worked it. "Well, I've been sitting here, watching you work in deep concentration, and surprise! You're almost Kivlanian!"

"I knew you were a charmer the second I laid eyes on you, Dara."

She giggled in spite of herself. "Well, it occurred to me, this is pretty nice. You're almost a good guy when you're just working hard, not acting like some jerk in a bar. So, it made me curious. Why is a guy like you, an obvious genius, almost retarded when it comes to women?"

"Arrested development," he replied, purring in ecstasy as she rubbed away. the knot in his shoulder. "I'm not kidding, Dara. I started college when I was barely out of diapers. Now that might impress some people, but I *hated* it. I got my third doctorate just when I hit puberty. I start noticing girls, they're all ten years older than I am. You know what college is like when you're only ten years old? It's like the whole world is having a wonderful party, and I'm the only one not invited, standing outside in the cold with my nose pressed up against the window. Goddamn, all I wanted was a girlfriend!"

She felt for him at once, but asked, "You're not scamming me, are you?"

"I never scam anyone, Dara. I never asked to be smart. I never wanted to start college as a nipper. I just wanted to do what other kids did. That was taken away from me. But they couldn't take away the fact that I liked women, and believe me, they tried. Anyway, enough about me, what about you?"

"I'm pretty normal," she said.

"How come you're not married? You're beautiful, you're smart, you're the vice president!"

"Never had the time. I was in the Air Force for ten years, I met Grig, and he suggested I go into politics, so I ran for a seat. Once you get into the legislature, you don't have time for anything else."

"Nonsense! There's always time for love."

"You're not in love."

"No, but I never stop hoping for it." He paused and looked dreamily out the window. "Could you imagine that? Waking up in the morning next to someone? You both open your eyes, look over at each other, laugh because you're so happy to see one another, the first thing to begin your day. You turn to each other and hug, kiss, say, 'Good morning, babe. I love you.' Could you imagine starting your day like that, every morning for the rest of your life? I mean, a lot of people do, and it just amazes me."

Dara took her hands from his shoulders. "Okay, shut up. Right now."

"I guess you have imagined it."

"This is Velax control, are you there, Minister?"

"Ready to go, Velax."

"Vidare, this is Prime Minister Junra."

"Evening, Prime Minister, this is Minister of Science Dacos, standing by with the vice president."

"Vice President, Minister, Velax thanks you. We are ready to reconfigure."

"Upload ready, Prime Minister."

"Upload initiated."

"Prime Minister, this process will be long and boring. We're talking three, maybe four minutes. Mind if I put on some music?"

"Go ahead, Minister. Make it sweet."

Ted actuated a copy of the Earth singer that Grig Holma had given him.

"What in the world is that, Vidare?" the Velaxian prime minister asked.

"It's, uh, Earth music."

"What are those instruments? I've never heard anything like it!"

"Don't know, Prime Minister. But it does get your attention, doesn't it?"

"What kind of song is it? Do you have any idea of what he's singing about?" Dara asked. "And I've never heard a voice like that! It's not a great voice, or a beautiful voice, but it's somehow . . . quite wonderful."

"Grig let me download their language when we first received their package," Ted said. "But it'll probably lose a lot in the translation."

"Come on, Vidare," the Velaxian prime minister needled him, "what's he singing about?"

"It's a love song," Ted replied.

"A love song!" Dara exclaimed. "But it sounds so happy! It's almost . . . exuberant!"

"Love can be happy, can't it? He's saying . . . uh, 'I have you beneath my outer skin layer.' "

"Ugh!" the prime minister and the vice president remarked in concert.

"It's obviously a metaphor," Ted said. " 'I have you in my heart, you and I are as one . . . but someone keeps calling me an idiot because I can't be victorious . . . but, nevertheless, I have you beneath my outer skin layer . . .' "

"Well," Dara remarked, "the words are pretty stupid but the singer and the music are just marvelous."

"Something tells me the words are pretty damned good," Ted replied. "We just don't understand them. Hmm. 'I've got you under my skin.' There's probably an entire vernacular working there."

"Upload completed, Vidare."

"Got you, Prime Minister. Test it well before you engage it."

"Thank you, Vidare. Say, uh, this is . . . unofficial, but do you think you could, uh . . ."

"Uploading a copy of it now, Prime Minister."

"Thank you, Vidare! Who is this guy again?"

"Your guess is as good as mine, sir. How would you pronounce this? Fr-an-ak Seena-tara? Damned if I know."

"Well, who cares? He's terrific. Thanks again. Velax out."

"Okay, next victim."

"That'll be Urno," Dara replied. "Ted, do you suppose . . ."

"Oh, you'll love this next one, Dara. It's a little sad, but lovely. Very little vernacular here. It's about a guy trying to leave very quietly so that his love won't wake up, because if she does, and holds out her arms, that'll be it—he'll never be able to go . . ."

EIGHT

MERAN Topak, a junior admiral from the nation of Ruud, was an intelligent and resourceful officer, but had not achieved high rank at an early age because he was being groomed for command. He had achieved this rank because he was exactly what great commanders needed—someone born to be *second*-in-command.

Therefore, while Meran Topak was both a disciple and a loyal assistant to Admiral Ro Heelvar, he was not, as many people assumed, his protégé. Another officer in such a position might have been angry, and it might have driven others to vengeance, but in reality, it suited Meran Topak just fine. Unlike most people who assume high rank, Topak was always happy, and even pleasantly surprised, to find himself exactly where he was.

Topak was that rarest of Kivlanian and human specimens—a man who knew his own limitations and was content nonetheless. And within those limitations, he was the best at what he did.

Therefore, when Vice Admiral Ro Heelvar called him

and informed him of "an opportunity" that the off-line processors had created, Topak did not question it. There was no need. He trusted Heelvar and was flattered that the admiral would be depending on him for so much. He vowed not to let him down.

ON Earth, Niz Elsev might have been a soccer mom. She spent all of her nonworking hours caring for her seven children, ferrying them to games, lessons, and amusements. She and her husband, despite their respective professional successes, believed that their real lives began when they arrived at home at the end of the day.

But on this particular evening, Niz Elsev's office intruded on her sacred home life in the most troubling way imaginable. For Niz Elsev was the brilliant young Velaxian admiral whose tactical genius had brought her fleet such an easy victory at the Crevan War Games.

Niz had never expected to achieve staff rank in the Velaxian Navy. She had not even graduated from the naval staff college in Vidare, where prospective officers from Velax's small Navy were trained. A graduate in architecture, she had applied for a direct commission when she and her husband were first married and they needed a steady paycheck while his own career was getting off the ground. Although she found the Navy agreeable employment and decided upon it as a career early on, she cheerfully accepted the fact that a nonacademy officer could realistically expect to go no further than the middle ranks, especially in a Navy as small as that of Velax. That was fine with her; the job offered security, and despite her husband's eventual success, they still had a large family and remembered their tough early days too vividly to ever completely trust their present good times.

When Niz made her decision to stay in the Navy, it was a simple choice. She had opted for the steady employment of a civil service job—a job that would offer stability and benefits, and yet one that wasn't especially taxing, which would give her plenty of time off to care for her growing family. But what she didn't expect, and what utterly stunned her, was the discovery that she had an incredible gift for the art of naval warfare.

Niz couldn't understand her success. To her, it was all so obvious. Once you considered logistics, weaponry, supply lines, fuel consumption, fleet dispositions, and speed, it all came together. All you had to do was keep the opposing fleet off-balance and stay a few steps ahead. You dictated the battle, not your opponent. If you act, then your enemy must react—so plan your actions accordingly. Once you did that, it was just a matter of time before he sailed right into your trap. What was the problem?

Apparently—as a kindly senior admiral explained to her when her career began its dramatic upward surge—it *wasn't* obvious to everyone else. The strategies that came to her in the bathtub or when she was changing the baby did not visit everyone else with the same clarity or regularity. Like it or not, he told her, she was special, and it was high time she got used to the idea. She became the youngest Velaxian admiral in five hundred years, and even that didn't count because back then wealthy parents were able to purchase commissions and promotions for their sons and daughters

It was all a little scary because it was far more than she ever wanted and nothing she had ever expected. What scared her the most, she admitted only to herself, was that the dynamic between her and Pel had changed, however subtly. Ever since they had met in college, Pel had been the star, the one who was going to make it and make it big. She would act in support, taking a stressless, bread-and-butter job as backup while Pel went out and conquered the world. And so he had; his amusement complex development firm became a huge success. But then her true talents suddenly emerged. It seemed that almost overnight she went from being an anonymous midgrade desk officer with no future to being the brightest star in the service. For the first time, she was the center of attention and Pel was the dutiful spouse. How would Pel take it? It worried her into insomnia until she found out that she truly *had* married a star. For it turned out that Pel not only was overcome with pride at her accomplishments but had fallen in love all over again and deeper than ever, as this completely new and exciting dimension of his wife emerged.

It made them the best kind of happy—older and wise enough to fully appreciate their good fortune with each other, and no longer kids but still young enough to do something about it.

Things were primed to go just wonderfully from here on in. The kids' college wouldn't break them after all, and they might even be able to retire a few years earlier than they had originally planned. And thus far, it wasn't working out too badly. She was appalled by the debacle in Creves after the war games, but her future was brighter than ever, with her pleased superiors hinting rather broadly that another promotion was in the works for her. She and Pel had moved the kids into a gigantic, beautiful new house in a suburb near the capital and life was truly wonderful. Or it would be for about another five minutes.

IN preparation for Global Feast Day, Niz and Pel were busy in the kitchen working the replicators overtime as they laid in the next day's meals. There were nine mouths to feed, but they had a system: she punched in the thought codes and he set them all up for MedCentral analysis. They would spend the next day in the pool, playing games and enjoying snacks—a real summer family holiday.

That was until Ro Heelvar and Meran Topak showed up at their door. Heelvar was the vice admiral of the Gaiusian Navy, and Topak, a bright younger officer like herself, was Niz's opposite number in the fleet of Ruud. The three had been the prime movers in the glorious victory in the recent war games. But on this day, both were wearing civilian clothes and something in their manner filled Niz with dread.

"Pel? You know Admiral Heelvar of Gaius and Admiral Topak of Ruud."

"Gentlemen, nice to see you again," he replied, shaking their hands. "Well, I'm sure you must have a lot to discuss, so I'll leave you to it. Admiral," he added, kissing his wife before leaving the room.

"Nice guy," Heelvar said.

"I like him," Niz replied. "Ro, what's all this about? Why aren't you with your families?"

"Something's come up, Niz, and we need your help."

Niz couldn't imagine what could have possibly come up since leaving the office that afternoon that would require urgent action on the part of the three navies, but she kept that to herself.

"Well, we are allies, fellows. How can I help?"

"We've got a marvelous opportunity here, Niz," Meran Topak said. "The kind that never, ever comes along."

Alarm bells went off in Niz's head, but she kept her features neutral. "I'm all for opportunities, Meran. What've you got?"

"A chance for you to really use your talents, Niz."

"I thought I already did. We won the war games, didn't we? I mean, you guys know I'm not conceited, but I did have something to do with that."

"Yes, and well done. But what would you say to . . . field command of the largest and most powerful fleet in the world?"

Niz's stomach turned over but she did her best to hide it.

"Vidare? Why would they give me command of their fleet?"

"Not Vidare," Ro Heelvar said firmly. "The Gaiusian

Empire. It would include Ruud and Velax to begin with, and later absorb Vidare and Urno. Maybe Lepang and Siga."

She leaned against the window. "Wow. Guys, I'm speechless. Hell of a challenge, though. I mean, what if Vidare and the other countries . . . what if they don't *want* to join the Gaiusian Empire?"

"That's where you come in," Ro answered. "Look, everybody's going off-line tomorrow for reconfiguration. But the three of us—we know the codes for our fleets. So what if everybody else is off-line, and we're not?"

"It's ours for the taking," Meran said. "As long as you come up with a battle plan."

"A battle plan for what?" Niz asked.

"A battle plan," Ro said, "to destroy the Vidarean Navy."

She nodded, as if deep in thought. These guys are *nuts*! "Hmm," she said. "I can do that easily enough. But what's the point? They still have the biggest army in the world and the biggest air force. And they have allies. So I take out their navy, so what? They launch their aircraft and bomb us back into the Wood Age."

"No, they won't," Ro Heelvar replied smugly.

"Why the hell not? We've just given them a good reason."

"Because while you're doing that, we turn south and take Lepang. Lepang falls, we roll into Siga and Urno. Now we're bigger than Vidare. We isolate them militarily and economically."

"What do they give a shit?" she demanded irritably. "They have everything they need. Then they rebuild their navy and I have to go back and do it again." She deliberately softened her tone. "You understand, gentlemen, I have to ask these questions. Success depends upon your answers."

"That's what makes you the best, Niz," Meran said.

"Okay," Niz began, "let's review. You want me to take

the combined fleet out tonight, figure I'll be within range of Vidare's naval base by late afternoon tomorrow. I take 'em out, and while I'm doing that, you're invading Lepang and hopefully Siga if all goes well. With their navy out of commission, Vidare can't send troops to reinforce Lepang or Siga, so we force them to the negotiating table. May I hazard a guess, that while we're at the negotiating table, since now we have a navy and they don't, we send an invasion force to Vidare, just to make sure they negotiate to our satisfaction?"

Meran smiled guiltily. "I knew you'd get it."

Niz clapped her hands in glee. *"I love it!"*

The two men nodded at each other.

"Okay, guys, I've got a lot of work to do. And I've got to break it to my family that I won't be here tomorrow, you bastards."

"Yeah, sorry about that, Niz," Ro said sympathetically.

"Like you care. Meet me at the admiralty later tonight and we'll firm this up. Grand admiral, huh? And what does that make you?"

Ro spread his hands. "Well, I was thinking, maybe, king . . . but president will do."

She hugged them both at the door and bid them good night. Then she closed the door behind them and slid to the floor. Who *were* those guys? She had known them, worked with them, for years. Their careers had paralleled. She had met their wives when they were just hopeful dates. Celebrated the births of their children. And now they were . . . strangers.

"Pel. Pel!"

Her husband came running in. "Niz? Niz! Are you all right?"

"All I wanted was a nice, secure, civil service job," she babbled. "That's all. Didn't want to bring the office home, didn't want to worry about company politics, sales records, keeping clients happy . . . so I joined the damned Navy . . ."

Pel sat on the floor beside her and rocked her in his arms.

"Pel . . . Pel, I love you so much . . ."

"It's okay, honey."

"It's not okay. Pel, get me my diary, now!"

Without protest, Pel jumped up and ran to their bedroom. He wished she could share her trouble with him, but he guessed it had to do with national security. Still, he couldn't imagine why she was so upset.

He brought her the diary. She placed the custom-shaped unit against her forehead and closed her eyes. There were tears streaming down her cheeks, and when she was done, the diary was streaked and damp.

She took her husband's face into her hands. "Pel. I have to go. I've been recalled to the fleet."

"Aw, damn it, honey—"

"Listen to me. If you don't hear from me in forty-eight hours, upload the diary to the media."

"What? Niz, what's going—"

"You know I can't tell you. Just—will you do that?"

"You know I will. But where are you—"

"Tell the children I love them."

"You can tell them yourself," he replied, really frightened now.

"There's no time. Pel. I loved you from the first time I saw you."

"At the student union? When I bumped into you—"

She smiled sadly. "No. I saw you twice before that. I tried to meet you but . . . it didn't happen. So I deliberately let you bump . . . into me."

"You did?"

"I've got to go."

"Niz!"

"I love you, Pel."

*   *   *

ADMIRALS Ro Heelvar and Meran Topak parted at the entrance to the Gaiusian Embassy.

"Can we trust her?" Meran asked.

"Who cares?" Ro snorted. "If we can, then she takes out the Vidarean Navy. And if we can't, she's out of the way, halfway across the ocean. We can't lose."

"I hope you're right."

"Of course I'm right. See you in Lepang."

NIZ Elsev took three separate public transport lines and two hired private cars to get to Embassy Row downtown. The streets were uncharacteristically empty as everyone was home peparing for Feast Day, which would make it easier for her to spot a tail if there was one.

She stayed close to the shadows as she neared the Vidarean Embassy. A lone, unarmed guard stood outside. She sneaked up behind him and placed her personal weapon to his head.

"I don't want to hurt you," she said. "Turn around, slow."

The guard, older and experienced, did exactly as ordered. He knew that as soon as he left his post, an alarm would go off inside the embassy guardroom, and his every movement would be traced.

"Just do as I say, and nothing will happen."

"You got it," the guard replied.

"Do you know who I am?"

"Yes, ma'am, Admiral."

"Get me inside. Now."

The guard was savvy enough to figure out that she meant via the guards' entrance and not the main doors.

When they got inside, the military attaché was waiting with an armed escort.

"Admiral Elsev?" the attaché could barely keep the note of surprise out of his voice.

"Sorry about this, Colonel," she said, pocketing her

weapon. "But I had to get in here fast and without being seen."

"What can I do for you, Admiral?"

"I need a secure comm-line to the president, and I need it now."

"That's a tall order, Admiral. The president—"

"Will be damned glad I contacted him. Just set it up, Colonel. I'm a little pushed for time."

GRIG Holma listened to Niz Elsev with growing alarm. He stared down at his desk and then back up at her holographic image.

"Admiral? You're sure?"

"Come on, Mr. President. Would I be here if I weren't?"

"Ro Heelvar," he muttered in disbelief. "How could he even think of such a thing?"

"With all due respect, sir," Niz snapped, "there'll be time for recriminations later. Right now, I need your help . . . as you need mine."

"Of course, Admiral, you are quite correct," he replied without rancor. Niz Elsev's reputation preceded her, and he was actually pleased to see that she seemed to be living up to it. "What do you suggest?"

"Can you mobilize five divisions in secret and airdrop them to support Lepang's defense force by morning?"

"It'll be tight. But in secret?"

"Just the mobilization, sir. The airdrop can have a thousand-piper band attached to it for all I care."

"I see, Admiral. And what about the naval battle?"

"Sir, put me on to the grand admiral. I'll handle the naval end of it. Please, sir, there isn't much time."

"All right," Grig Holma replied, trying to fight the benumbed feeling that was taking him over. How could he have been so foolish, so naive? How could he have forgotten that no one was perfect, that *someone* would take advantage of a world with its defenses completely down? Just because there hadn't been a war in three hundred years, did that mean that belligerence and ambition no longer existed?

This would be stopped, he promised himself. And then, when the crisis was over, he would resign. The people of Vidare deserved better. Dara would make a wonderful president. But first he had to get through the next few days without destroying the world as he knew it . . . and loved it.

NINE

"**ALL** hands to the bridge," Matt Wiener ordered.

"What's going on?" Bob Rodgers asked grumpily. He hoped it was important. Rodgers had had trouble sleeping in space, and although Doralee Conger-Levin had at first dispensed him sleeping pills, she had soon ceased to do so, not wanting to create a real or imagined dependence upon them. She had since allowed him nothing stronger than herbal tea, which he had never liked. Irregular sleep was making him grouchy, and other members of the crew tried not to disturb him if it was at all possible.

"We have a visual," Matt said.

The crew gathered at the bridge for a view of the planet from near-orbit.

"It doesn't look all that different," Claude Monroe said.

"Yeah, it *is* round," Butch Caldwell replied. Claude smacked his shoulder. The Virginia aristocrat and the former Brooklyn gangbanger had become good friends after five months in space.

But the planet did resemble Earth. There were white

wisps partially obscuring large patches of green over a larger sea of blue.

"It's beautiful," Doralee said. "It's like home."

"Okay," Matt said. "Jeanne? How about those missiles they fired at the *Lifespring*?"

"I have them, Matt. It's a drogue space platform, uninhabited."

"Lock in the coordinates. Any movement at all, blast it. John? Surface activity?"

John Ryham held up his hand. "Captain, this is very strange. I've been monitoring the surface since last night, and all was quiet. But in the last hour there has been . . . my God! Massive naval movement westward and what seems to be a gigantic airborne armada moving eastward."

"Jeanne?" Matt asked his second-in-command. "What do you think?"

"It could be a prelude to World War III down there, Matt. This could prove to be a bad time for a visit."

"Open a frequency," he ordered. Jeanne complied, using the communications codes recorded by the *Lifespring*. "It's open, Captain," Jeanne said.

"This is Captain Matt Wiener of the Earth ship USS *Forlorn Hope* calling the planet Kivlan. Will the nation of Vidare please respond?"

There was no answer.

"This is *Forlorn Hope*, come in, Vidare."

"Maybe they're a little preoccupied, Matt," Claude said.

"You're probably right," Matt replied. "Okay, Vidare, in your own good time. We'll be here. *Forlorn Hope* out."

THE commander of the Vidarean Air Force Space Monitoring Division contacted Grig Holma immediately.

"Mr. President? Colonel Vayo, space monitoring control."

"I'm a little busy right now, Colonel."

"This is important, sir. The Earth ship, Mr. President. It has returned."

Grig resisted the impulse to groan out loud. "Play the transcript."

"Yes, sir."

Grig listened to the recording of Matt Wiener's hail. He could tell immediately that this commander was different from the last, confident and businesslike. He especially respected the captain's patience.

"What do you think, Colonel?"

"Sir, it's just a guess based on a short hail, but I would say that this fellow knows what he's doing. He's not pushing us, he obviously knows there's something brewing here on the surface, and he's happy to allow us to give it precedence, sir. And there's something else."

"And that is . . .?"

"I don't think this one will scare easily, sir. Our orbital missile platform? He's got a lock on it, sir. Some kind of weapon system, it has to be. I think that if we try to put one across *his* bow, he'll blow it to bits before we get a shot off."

"Are you saying they're here to fight, Colonel?" Grig asked, not adding, That'd be just what we'd need right now.

"No, sir. The ship is armed, but we detect no enabling of weapons. Just the lock on the missile platform."

"I guess I'd better talk to them, then," Grig sighed.

"It might be a good idea, sir."

"Set up the link and notify me when it's ready." He closed the channel and called his secretary. "Have the vice president and the minister of science report here immediately. That's right. Immediately."

NIZ Elsev stood at the bridge of the Velaxian flagship, the *Roana Pri*. The battle cruiser, five times the size of an American aircraft carrier and as many times as fast, plowed through the waves, leading a 110-ship armada on a breakneck course toward the Vidarean capital.

"Admiral," the *Roana Pri*'s captain reported, "four more hours until we are within range of Vidare."

"Thank you, Captain."

"Uh, ma'am?"

"Captain?"

The captain was about to ask what it was they were doing, why they were steaming at flank speed toward the homeland of their greatest ally on the one day in history when that ally would be completely vulnerable. Then he suddenly decided against it. He would be told when the admiral saw fit to tell him.

"Would you like anything from the mess, Admiral?"

Niz turned to the captain and understood immediately.

"When the time comes, Captain, I'll let you know."

"Very well, ma'am." The captain then left the bridge, went to his stateroom, and retrieved his personal sidearm. If the admiral was planning what he thought she was planning, he wasn't going to let it happen without a fight.

"**ATTENTION.** *Forlorn Hope*, this is Vidare control. Are you there, *Forlorn Hope?*"

The voice, not a metallic reproduction, sounded as if it was phonetically pronouncing a language it didn't understand. Nevertheless, it was the first real contact from another planet, and each crew member felt a sudden rush of emotion.

"Vidare control, this is Captain Wiener of the *Forlorn Hope*, go ahead," Matt responded after a long pause.

"Captain, this is Colonel Stava Vayo of the Vidarean Air Force Space Monitoring Division," a halting transmission began. "Please forgive the long pauses in our conversation—I have to wait for your words to be translated through our comm-data banks, then respond in my own language, then wait for the phonetic translation, which I am reading to you now."

The crew looked at each other and nodded approvingly. This Vayo seemed like their kind of guy. A soldier who gets it done. And why should that be surprising? There was a bond between soldiers of all nations; why not from other planets as well? Weren't the demands and the requirements of character universal?

"That's quite all right, Colonel, take all the time you need. It's a pleasure to be speaking with you."

"Thank you, Captain. Sir, I will be turning you over to President Holma now."

"Very well, Colonel. I hope we meet soon."

A new voice came on the channel. There were no pauses this time. The voice at first spoke with an almost–Central European accent that gradually faded as the conversation went on and Grig picked up pronounciation cues from Matt's Southern California accent.

"Captain Wiener? I am Grig Holma."

"Mr. President? I'm honored. Uh, sir, if you don't mind my asking, you don't sound as though you are reading from a phonetic translation."

"Very good, Captain. I am not. I have learned your language, thanks to the materials in your predecessor's package. The ability to assimilate new languages easily, you will discover, is a particularly Kivlanian trait. Although I imagine my accent and grammar may render my speech, at times, incomprehensible. I apologize in advance for any such instance."

"Not all, sir. You speak our language quite well."

"Captain, the other ship . . . I trust no one was hurt? I assure you that was not our intention."

"A few bruised egos, sir. But that action did cause us grave concern."

"And for that I apologize. Be assured that Kivlan's greatest desire is peace."

"With all due respect, Mr. President, from what we can

see from up here, things don't look all that peaceful down there."

"You may have a point, Captain. Unfortunately, I do not have the time to fully explain myself at the moment."

"Understood, Mr. President."

Ted Dacos tapped Grig on the shoulder. "I'll go up there, Grig. I'll use the repair ship and dock with them."

"I'll go, too," the vice president said.

"I can't spare you," Grig told her.

"Please. I'm ex–Air Force, remember? I'm qualified to pilot and dock the repair ship. It's been a while, but—"

Grig nodded. "Very well. Captain? I am completely out of time. However, we will be sending two representatives up there to meet you. Our vice president, Dara Widh, and our minister of science, Trazor Dacos, will dock with your vessel in . . . twenty minutes?"

Ted shook his head.

"Thirty minutes. Is that satisfactory?"

"Yes, Mr. President. We'll make them as welcome as we can."

"Thank you, Captain. Colonel Vayo will be contacting you to brief you on docking procedures. Vidare out."

Matt turned to the crew. "I hope everyone brought along a Class-A uniform? We're about to have some very important visitors."

"*TED*, are you sure this is a good idea?"

Ted Dacos regarded the president with a shrug. "I don't care one way or another. I want to meet these people."

"Dara?"

"Grig, it's the opportunity of a lifetime. You should really be the one to go. But since you can't, the responsibility falls to me."

"Well, be careful up there, you two. Will you be armed?"

"Absolutely not," Dara replied firmly.

"Are you sure that's a good idea? I've read these people's history. They're animals."

Ted Dacos waved his hand at the sit-map spanning an entire wall of the room. A huge formation of aircraft was moving eastward toward Lepang, while a giant naval armada was heading rapidly toward Vidare.

"Yeah, well, so are we. We ought to get along just fine."

BOB Rodgers, who had the most experience as a docking officer, albeit under the sea with DSRVs, was put in charge of the linkup with the Vidarean repair ship. Everyone else crowded in at the portholes for their first look at an extraterrestrial space vehicle.

They were somewhat disappointed. All had grown up on popular fiction and expected a darkly dramatic spacecraft with sharp, swept lines and aggressively pointed engine pods. But the Vidarean ship was as about exciting to look at as a Ford Taurus. It was dirtied-white, squared-off, and utilitarian, not particularly aerodynamic and rather beaten up. But it was not of Earth and that gave it significance.

The docking went smoothly, just a soft kiss between the two ships, followed by the extension of a docking collar over the aft hatch.

The entire complement of the *Forlorn Hope* stood to attention, the three command officers composing the front rank. Matt Wiener and Bob Rodgers wore their dress whites; Claude Monroe, his Class-A greens; and the remaining crew had all donned their respective Air Force blues.

Since the crew of the *Forlorn Hope* did not have a tape of the Vidarean national anthem—or even know if they had one—a compact disc comprising a shortened medley of "The Star-Spangled Banner," "God Save the King," and "La Marseillaise" was punched in as the airlock hissed open.

The vice president entered through the lock, followed

by the minister of science. The crew had not known what to expect, but the sight of two rather normal-looking people was initially disappointing. They walked on two legs, had two regular arms, and had a head and body all very much in proportion. They were hardly lizardlike or grasshopperish, or even a skewed, bizarre version of humans. All they were was foreign rather than extraterrestrial; and once foreigners became familiar, they ceased to be foreigners at all.

From the front rank, Jeanne-Marie Fournier glanced back at Doralee Conger-Levin with a slight grin. There was nothing extraterrestrial about this guy—he was hot! He was smaller than medium height and rather slender, but with the wiry and suggestive grace of a Flamenco dancer. His hair was a natural sea-turquoise and his skin was smooth-shaven bottle green. Foreign and alien perhaps, but not all that different; and from the subtle glance with which he regarded them, they weren't all that different—or unattractive—either.

The first extraterrestrial flirt in history had taken place.

There was equally subtle communication between the men of the *Forlorn Hope*. Matt Wiener knew an intimate thing or two about extremely good-looking female members of the executive branch of government, and this vice president was certainly in a league with Ann Catesby. She was taller than the male, her skin a lighter shade of the green and her hair a darker blue. There was a visible discoloration on the left side of her neck, a rash of some sort. But her features were intra- rather than extraterrestrial.

"They look like us," Dara whispered to Ted Dacos. "Incredible!"

"Not so incredible," Ted whispered back.

The Vidareans and the Terrans stood regarding each other as the American, British, and French anthems played out. Then all stood frozen for a moment until Matt Wiener broke the pregnant silence.

"*Forlorn Hope*, salute. To." Matt stepped forward. "Ms. Vice President, Minister, welcome aboard the USS *Forlorn Hope*. I am Captain Matthew Wiener, United States Navy, at your service."

Dara nodded at this polite, unintelligible greeting and glanced at Ted.

"What'd he say?" she asked him out of the side of her mouth.

"He's welcoming us on board," Ted whispered back. "Thank . . . you . . . Captain," Ted said haltingly. "May I pre-sent Vice President Dara Widh."

"Ma'am," Matt nodded.

"Tell him the president sends his compliments and regrets not being here to greet them personally," Dara said.

The crew was listening carefully, instinctively trying to discern the slightest resemblance of the Vidarean language to that of any on Earth. There was none.

"The president sends his apologies for not being here to greet you personally," Ted translated, gaining confidence in his English. "I am Ted Dacos. Welcome to Kivlan." Ted looked questioningly at the Earth crew, who had suddenly registered expressions of surprise.

"Begging your pardon, Minister," Matt said. "Did you say your name was . . . *Ted*?"

Dacos smiled knowingly. "A strange name on Kivlan, as well. My initials, you see."

Matt smiled. "Not a strange name on Earth, sir. A rather common one, at that."

Ted's eyes widened. He turned to Dara. "It seems that 'Ted' is a common Earth name," he told her.

"I think we'll find that we're more alike than not," she replied, looking at the two women of the crew. She could see that both took pride in their appearance. The one in the front rank was tall, slender, dark brown in color, and had a bearing that bordered on the regal. The one behind her was a delicate pale, more petite, rather voluptuous, and golden-haired, somewhat older but still very pretty.

How strange, Dara thought to herself. I am the vice president of a powerful nation, meeting extraterrestrials and making history—yet what I'd really like to do is talk to these two women about their beauty secrets. How does the light one get her hair to shine so? What is the secret of the dark one's beautiful skin? It had been a long time since Dara had just sat and talked of nothing with other women, and she suddenly realized how much she had missed it. In an odd but serious way, she wanted to become friends with these two women.

"Sir," Matt Wiener was saying, "May I present my crew?"

"By all means," Ted replied.

"Sir, my first officer, Major Jeanne-Marie Fournier of the *Armée de l'Air* of the nation of France. My second officer, Major Claude Monroe, United States Marine Corps. Our flight surgeon, Lieutenant Colonel Doralee Conger-Levin, United States Air Force; Lieutenant Bob Rodgers, United States Navy; Flight Lieutenant John Ryham, Royal Air Force of the nation of Great Britain; and Captain Butch Caldwell, United States Air Force."

"All but two of the crew are from a nation called the United States," Ted whispered to Dara. "That must be Earth's Vidare."

"I think this historic meeting calls for a toast," Matt declared.

"With what?" Claude wanted to know. "Tang?"

"Excuse me." Matt disappeared for a few moments, leaving everyone else in an awkward silence. Doralee Conger-Levin, deciding the hell with it—she was a doctor, after all—picked up her medical bag and approached the vice president. She bowed slightly and placed her hand to her neck. Dara, slightly embarrassed, instinctively pulled her collar up to cover the rash caused by the fallout.

Doralee smiled kindly and turned to Ted. "I'm a doctor," she began. "I think I can help ease her discomfort."

"The doctor thinks she might have something for your fallout rash," Ted said to Dara.

"Oh!" Dara replied, smiling. Dara motioned for Doralee to go ahead. The flight surgeon reached into her bag and took out a tube of aloe-based medical cream. She looked inquiringly at the vice president, who nodded her assent to proceed. The aloe cream felt wonderfully cool against her skin and made the itching cease immediately. Her grin of relief needed no translation.

Dara reached out and touched the flight surgeon's hair. She was surprised when the doctor emitted a chuckle. "It's not me, not anymore," she said to Ted Dacos. "Thank God for Paul Mitchell!"

Ted began to translate, but Dara understood that as well. She was beginning to like these Earth people.

Matt returned carrying a bottle and a short stack of plastic cups.

"Napoleon brandy," he said. "I figured we might run into an occasion that would call for it."

"That's contraband," Claude said.

"Oh, please," Matt groaned. "I thought political correctness went out thirty years ago."

"So it did," Claude replied, taking the cups from Matt and handing them around.

When everyone's glass was filled, Matt raised his glass. "To peace and friendship," he toasted.

"Peace and friendship," everyone repeated, including Dara, who stated the unfamiliar words haltingly. No one drank, however, as they were waiting for the senior Vidarean to respond in kind.

"Yse hvenesa," she declared.

"Eternal kindness," Ted translated, pleased that the Earth people seemed moved by Kivlan's ancient, simple, and elegant toast.

"Yse hveneesa," the Earth crew replied.

Dara and Ted sniffed experimentally at their glasses,

and then took small sips. *"Desada!"* They both said approvingly.

"Desada," Matt said. "Brandy. Napoleon, the best in the world."

"Of course it is," Jeanne said. "It's French."

"You must try our Vidarean desada," Ted said to her.

"I look forward to it, Minister."

"Now, none of that," Ted said. "Call me Ted. Our planet seldom stands on ceremony."

Jeanne noticed that his English was rapidly becoming clearer and less accented. "How did you learn our language so quickly?"

"It is a Kivlanian gift," he replied. "Early in our history we were made aware of the importance of communication—and the tragedy of miscommunication. Everyone on our planet speaks at least three or four languages; therefore, everyone can communicate with everyone else. No single country wallows in isolation. That is why we are by and large a peaceful race."

"If I may, Minister—that doesn't appear to be the case at the moment. "If it's not too much trouble, could you fill us in on what's going on?" Matt asked. "Maybe we can help."

"I'll give you a brief overview," Ted replied. "But I don't think you should get involved."

THE Roana Pri was nearing the point of no return; soon the fleet would be within threat range of the Vidarean naval base.

The captain of the *Roana Pri* stepped carefully up to the bridge, edging silently behind the admiral. His sidearm was pointed low and at the deck.

Admiral Niz Elsev turned and faced him.

"Captain? Are you pulling that weapon on me?"

"With apologies, ma'am. I have no desire to harm you. But I am taking command and recalling the fleet. I beg

you, please do not resist. I know you have many children."

"I think we'd better talk, Captain."

"Fine, ma'am. As long as you keep your hands on the
rail where I can see them."

"As you wish, Captain, I . . ." Niz's blue skin paled.
She clutched her left arm and collapsed to the deck, her
eyes open and vacant.

"Admiral? Admiral!" The captain rushed over and knelt
beside her. "Admiral. Admiral Elsev! Are you—" He
leaned over and placed his ear to her breast. He suddenly
felt stunned by a leg-over kick to the back of his head.
Niz grabbed his weapon and scrambled up off the deck.

"I'm sorry about that, Captain, but I had no choice."

"Damn it, Niz, that really hurt, you know! It's not like
I'm a kid anymore."

"It's okay, Troka. I'm sorry I had to do that, but I'm
glad I found out where your loyalties really are. Can you
stand up?"

"Yeah, but I won't enjoy it a whole lot."

"Come on, I need you. We've got a lot of work ahead
of us."

TEN

"**MY** God," Matt said.

"The man is a maniac," Doralee remarked.

"I wish we could help," Butch Caldwell said.

There was a moment of tense silence, which then exploded into a series of urgings.

"C'mon, let's get down there, Matt!"

"It's a war we can stop before it begins, for Christ's sake!"

"We can help 'em turn these guys back!"

"C'maaaaahn! These are good people!"

"Let's go kick 'em in the ass! C'mon! Shit!"

"Whoa, whoa, *whoa!*" Matt silenced his crew. "May I remind you all that our brief here is to make contact—*not* to involve ourselves in a war about which we know nothing. Our mission is *peace*. Remember? Peace, love, Kumbaya? You know, Da-da-DA, da-da," he added to the tune of the greeting in *Close Encounters of the Third Kind*. "And, no offense meant, Ms. Vice President, Minister—but we have heard only one side of this issue."

"No offense taken, Captain," Ted replied. "Your caution is entirely understandable."

"Oh, come on, Matt," Claude argued. "You know these guys are right! How can we just stand here and let the whole plan—"

Matt made a cross of his forefingers, which he held in Claude's face. "Back! Back!" he shouted. "You're getting that psycho-Marine gleam in your eyes, Claude."

Ted regarded the puzzled look on Dara's face. "He's kidding," Ted whispered. "Sort of."

"Matt," John Ryham began. "Can't we just observe . . . or perhaps . . . advise? If not actually participate? Where's the harm in that?"

"The harm is, one of you could get killed," Matt said. "Your wife's having a baby, John. It'd be nice if I could bring you back to meet him. Or her. As for you, Claude—"

"Oh, puh-huh-leeze!" Claude exclaimed.

"What the hell's going on?" Dara whispered to Ted.

"They want to help us," Ted whispered back.

"They do? Why?"

"Apparently, they like us."

"Can't we take a vote?" Claude asked.

"Ex*cuse* me," Matt retorted. "What is this, the Mickey Mouse Club? We don't take votes; you follow orders." Matt held up his hands to calm everyone down. "Look, guys, I know you want to get down there and help out. Well, so do I. But we can't. We don't know enough about the situation. And to our new friends, please don't take this the wrong way, but we know nothing about your planet, the way it is run, who's right and who's wrong."

Ted translated quickly for Dara, who looked at Matt and nodded in understanding and approval. "A bright man, this captain," she said to Ted.

"Tactics," Butch piped up. "Can we at least help with tactics?"

"May I remind you, Butch," Matt said, "this is a highly

advanced planet that obviously has sophisticated military establishments of its own? Probably light-years ahead of ours? Why would they need our help?"

Dara, who had had the bulk of the exchange relayed to her by Ted, stepped forward. "My friends," she said as Ted translated for her. "Your kindness is . . . overwhelming. I hope that we may soon deepen our relationship. But your captain's prudence is well founded. This is not your fight. At least, not yet. We hope to bring this . . . difficulty . . . to a quick conclusion. But until then, please remain at a safe distance. You have come a long way and you are welcome. But this conflict is a Kivlanian problem. Please let us sort it out ourselves."

"Ms. Vice President." Bob Rodgers spoke for the first time. "This conflict . . . will there be many casualties?"

"Casualties?" she replied through Ted. "We can't afford casualties, Lieutenant. If even one Kivlanian dies because of this, it'll be a tragedy beyond anything we've ever known."

THE Captain of the *Roana Pri*'s jaw dropped. "My God, Niz," he gasped.

"Do you think we can pull it off?" she asked him.

"It's a gutsy plan, Niz. There's a lot that can go wrong."

"Tell me about it. But I'm glad you're on board, Troka. The plan, I mean. I'd hate to have to go it alone."

"CAPTAIN," Dara said haltingly after some coaching from Ted, "would you like to return to Vidare with us?"

"Can I bring some of my crew with me?"

"Yes."

He nodded his thanks. Then a thought struck him. "Vice President, Minister, I have to talk to you. You may not like what you hear."

Ted and Dara turned to look at each other. Then they accompanied Matt to the bridge.

"I have to be honest with you," he began with difficulty.

"Honesty is a good thing."

"Sometimes it's better to leave well enough alone, Minister. But I can't, in good conscience, accept your hospitality without coming clean."

Dara touched his hand and nodded for him to continue.

"When we heard that the *Lifespring*—the ship that was here before—was fired upon, it frightened us."

"That's what it was meant to do," Dara said. "For your own good."

"Yes, but we didn't know that. All we knew was that a planet with life like ours had initiated a hostile action against us. We knew nothing of your capabilities, and even less of your intentions. In other words, our biggest fear was that you would follow us back to Earth and . . . destroy us."

"That's preposterous!" Dara exclaimed.

"I know that now . . . but can you blame us?"

"Perhaps not," she admitted.

"Well, we had to make sure," Matt said. "That's the real reason for this visit."

Ted stared at Matt unblinkingly. "So, Matt," he said finally, "what would you have done if your fears were confirmed?"

"In all honesty, I can't say for certain what I would have done. I can only tell you what we are equipped to do."

"I know you have guns. You could have easily destroyed our orbital defense platform." His eyes narrowed. "I've read your history," he gasped. "You didn't—"

"I'm afraid it's true, Minister. None of us like the idea, but there it is." He translated for Dara.

She put her hand to her face in horror. "How could you?"

"I know now," Matt replied, his face falling. "I couldn't. 'I am become death,' " he quoted. "No, I couldn't."

Dara walked to him slowly and embraced him, placing her head on his right shoulder and then on his left. "I should be very angry. You didn't have to tell us," she said. "There was no way that we would have ever found out. That took courage . . . and character."

"Anyway," Ted said, "the point is moot. We couldn't have come after you even if we wanted to."

"You couldn't?"

"Never. You see, Matt, we don't have a space program."

"What?" Matt broke from Dara, stunned.

"It's true. That repair ship—that's it. And it can't leave orbit. The gun platform is for defense only, just in case."

"But you obviously have the intelligence," Matt replied. "Even the technology!"

"But not the interest or the desire," Ted said.

"I don't understand!"

"That's because you don't live on Kivlan," Dara replied.

MATT took Bob Rodgers and John Ryham aside. "I want the two of you to stay here. John, you've got the airplane; maintain a steady orbit. We'll get you down in the next shift if all goes well. If anything happens, though, I'm not leaving your kid without a father."

John hid his disappointment well. "Yes, sir."

"Bob?"

"Sir?"

"I've got a big job for you. I want it done fast and I want it done right."

"Of course, sir."

Matt took a deep breath. "Remove all of the warheads and store them in a separate isolation area."

"But, Matt, that's—"

"These people can't hurt us, Bob. And I won't take the chance of hurting them. We'll keep our guns on line just in case, but I want the teeth yanked out of those nukes. Do it. That's an order."

"Sixteen warheads? Where am I going to put them?"

"Flush 'em down the john for all I care. Just get them out. We're here to learn, not to destroy."

THE interior of the repair ship had all of the aesthetic attraction of a New York City subway car. It was about sixty feet long, with hard, polymer-like bench seating that ran down either side of the vessel. The pilot's station was merely a slightly more comfortable-looking chair facing front. There seemed to be no controls at all; no joystick or control panel was evident. Dara merely sat in the chair, strapped in, whispered something to no one in particular, and the vessel slowly disengaged from the docking collar. Then she whispered again and the vehicle dropped like an egg rolling off a high table. The effect was a bit disquieting until the ship engaged full power. Then there was hardly any sensation of movement at all.

"The vice president was an Air Force pilot before going into politics," Ted remarked, which earned approving nods from his guests.

Jeanne-Marie lightly nudged Matt. "Are you thinking what I'm thinking?"

Matt nodded slowly. "I'm wondering what powers this craft."

"And is your conclusion the same as my conclusion?"

"My God," Matt gasped.

"They've done it! Minister," Jeanne asked Ted, "What is the power source for this spacecraft?"

"I'm not sure what you would call it in your language. But we no longer use fuel. Our fuel source is . . . everywhere."

"Zero-point energy!" Jeanne exclaimed.

Ted nodded. "We made the discovery three hundred years ago—which is, not so coincidentally, when we had our last war."

"Imagine that," Jeanne said wondrously. "To be able to draw energy from anything . . . anywhere. No need for electric generators, nuclear power plants . . . no disputes over oil . . ."

"Kivlan must be a paradise," Butch said.

Ted shrugged. "I don't know if I would say that. There are no paradises in *this* life. There is only . . . home."

DARA dropped to a thousand feet and skimmed over the Vidarean Sea as they neared home. It was late evening but the city was lit almost as bright as day.

"Daribi, our capital," Ted said.

"It looks like Marina del Rey," Matt remarked in surprise, more to himself. "Or Mission Bay or La Jolla."

"It sure doesn't look like a sci-fi movie," Claude said.

It was true. Although some of the taller buildings had odd shapes that seemed to defy architectural stress postulates—some like lightning bolts and some round like the sun—most were simply tall and straight, and faced with glass or a gold sandstone. And the center of Vidare's capital city did look more like the wealthy marina district of a resort town than a center of bureaucracy, and that was exactly the way Vidareans liked it. There were also many simple houses, each with more land than would be expected within a city.

Dara circled to give everyone a better view.

"Sailboats!" Doralee exclaimed, thrilled. She had become a sailing aficionado in medical school in Miami. "You sail on this planet?"

"Of course we do," Ted replied. "Why wouldn't we? Look, there's our naval base. Off to your right." Matt strained to get a glimpse of the ships at anchor. They were uniformly sized and oval-shaped.

"You have a navy?" Butch asked, stunned.

"We've got oceans, of course we have navies. Almost every nation on Kivlan has one. Why should that be so odd?"

Butch turned to look at Claude and then Doralee, who were seated on either side of him. "Have you ever read a single sci-fi book or seen one sci-fi movie where another planet has a navy? I mean, they've always got rockets zooming around, but never—"

"Yes, but this is the real deal, Butch," Doralee replied. "I wonder . . . Minister? May I ask a question?"

"Of course . . . as long as you call me Ted."

"Thank you. What would you say is the defining characteristic of your planet?"

Ted grinned and nodded his head. "Interesting. Do you mean my planet . . . or the people on my planet?"

"Why, both, I suppose."

"The name Kivlan means 'tranquil,' and that is by and large correct, although I would add that this is also a generous planet. It has always given its inhabitants everything we've ever needed. Our people? That's a little more difficult. We've progressed far enough in our development to enjoy life . . . we simply don't need to struggle to survive anymore. Our economies provide full employment, and while not everyone is rich, no one is poor. No one goes without anything they need, or most things they could want. We like sports, theater, amusements . . . by and large, I guess you could call us people of leisure."

"Tell me you've ever heard of *that* before," Butch said to Claude. "When have you ever seen ETs *not* portrayed as a bunch of stiffs?"

"Hate to tell you this, sport," Claude whispered back, "but right now, *we're* the ones who are the ETs."

Dara banked the ship and reduced speed to little more than a hover. The Terrans on board noticed that they were over an unremarkable, squat-looking sandstone building. The roof was flat, and a figure of a sun on waves was carved into its surface.

"Executive House," Ted informed them. "Welcome."

"This is where your president lives?"

"Yes. We're very informal here on Kivlan."

"But where are the guards? Soldiers? Police?"

"Guards? Whatever for?"

"But anybody could just walk right in—"

"Yes, but they wouldn't. That would be most inconsiderate, really quite rude. And they can always make an appointment."

"Hey, wait a minute! What's that over there? Where all those people are waiting on line?"

Dara veered off from her course to Executive House and flew toward a small, freestanding building with a glass canopy over the front entrance. There was a large crowd waiting in line and milling about.

She smiled at Ted. "Gin-cha," she said.

He returned her smile. "That's the Gin-cha," he told his guests. "Probably the most popular club in Daribi."

"Club? You mean, like a nightclub?" Butch asked. "Music, dancing, that sort of thing?"

"Exactly."

The Terrans stared at each other in amused surprise and soon all were laughing, the laughter of familiarity.

"Sorry," Matt said, responding to quizzical looks from his hosts. "Something so mundane as this . . . standing on line outside a disco . . . it's all so incredible. It's such a . . . a touchstone! The things we have in common!" He sobered immediately. "Minister, I know this isn't the time, but we're going to need to know everything about you! How did your civilization develop? How did you evolve, physically, anthropologically? If it's quite all right, I'd like our flight surgeon to examine a Kivlanian, see just how much we really do have in common. And if it turns out that we are so much alike, then would it hold true for the entire universe? Are there any properties that your planet has that ours doesn't? Is there—"

"I know, I know," Ted replied, laughing. "A million questions. In due time, of course."

"I'm sorry I got a little carried away, but—" Matt stopped talking as the ship slowed to hover and began letting down on the roof of Executive House.

The craft touched down smoothly and without the slightest bump. Butch found himself watching Dara, and allowed himself a small nod of approval when he saw a look of satisfaction on her face; apparently, pilots *were* the same all over the universe. A sweet greaser of a landing gave a pilot as much to puff up about here as it did in Houston or at Edwards. Dara turned around and saw Butch looking at her. There was a hint of that wiseguy, hot-pilot, try-and-top-that-one-you-pudknocker grin on her lips, which made both of them chuckle self-consciously.

Matt thought that they would be exiting the craft on the roof, but at just that moment the craft began to sink. They had landed on a movable platform, which descended into what could only be described as a garage. There were a few approximate vehicles of varied design, but like the repair ship, rather boring to look at.

"Automobiles," Claude asked in suprise. "Do you—" He cut himself off as something out the window distracted him. A vehicle pulled slowly into the garage; as there were no wheels, it seemed to be held up on an air cushion. The door was opened for the driver by a young man, who then got into the car and zoomed over to a parking space.

"Get outta here!" Claude whooped. "This planet has . . . *valet parking?*"

THEY heard the bagpipe before they were halfway down the aqua-walled hallway to the executive office. The crew noted with interest the fact that this planet heavily favored bright pastel colors, further dispelling the notion of a foreign world as a dark, austere, and spartan place to dwell.

"I wish John were here," Butch said of his fellow crewman, who was half-Scottish. "He'd love this."

"I like it, too," Jeanne-Marie said.

"You do?" Butch asked in surprise.

"The French and the Scots go way back, Butch; don't you know your history? The Auld Alliance? Mary Queen of Scots was even Queen of France for a while."

"Here we are," Ted said, knocking once before opening the door.

The president placed his bagpipes on his desk and stood. He was an azure-colored giant, Jeanne noticed, well over six and a half feet tall, large-boned and somewhat heavily set, like a former NFL interior lineman going to fat. But there was an intelligence about him that was quite plain to see, as well as a certain . . . could it be *gentleness*?

"Mr. President, may I present the crew of the Earth ship *Forlorn Hope*?"

The president had himself introduced to each Terran individually. He had something to say to each of them, sometimes in halting, broken English, and sometimes translated by Ted Dacos. Is our atmosphere comfortable for you? Was your trip a long one? Have you eaten yet? Can you breathe all right?

But when he got to Jeanne-Marie Fournier, the president became shy and a little tongue-tied. Ted tried to cover for him by making up a translated question, but Jeanne-Marie, an extremely charismatic woman who had often affected men in such a way before, knew immediately what was happening. She thought it was the sweetest thing she had ever heard of. Out of the corner of her eye, she saw Doralee—and even more surprisingly, Dara Widh—look in her direction with eyes dancing merrily.

The president bowed a little awkwardly and turned to Matt. He's too shy to hit on me, Jeanne thought. How refreshing!

"Well," the president said, clearing his throat. "Things are somewhat hectic just now, but we should all eat. Why don't you all join me?" He took a deep breath and offered his arm to Jeanne-Marie. "Major?"

"Delighted, Mr. President."

"Oh, do call me Grig. So you are what is called . . . an *astro-naut*? What does that mean, exactly?"

"Star voyager," she replied.

"Star voyager!" he replied. "How—" He whispered something to Ted, who whispered something back. "How evocative! You must tell me all about it!"

"Now I've seen everything," Claude whispered to Butch.

"How do you mean?"

"This guy's the president, he's about to go to war, he's just seen aliens land on his planet . . . and he's goddamn *dating*!"

ELEVEN

BOTH Admiral Niz Elsev and First Captain Troka Dorig were standing at the rail, but they were plugged into the command center and ran the operation with salt spray blowing in their faces, the way they both preferred it.

Both wore small headsets that hooked them visually into the action, as if they were watching it on a transparent table. They had worked feverishly for the last few hours, and now all of their labor would either come to fruition or end in catastrophe.

Niz turned to Troka. "Come here," she said. He did so and she put her face up to his and kissed him. "Victory and peace."

He returned the kiss. "Victory and peace, Niz. I hope everyone's ready."

Niz thought about the quote from the Earth poet that someone had read to her many months ago, when the *Lifespring*'s communications package had first arrived on Kivlan. " 'All things are ready if our minds be so,' " she said. "Okay, let's hit it. Fire control! Are we in range?"

"Thirty seconds, ma'am." Through her headset, she could see as well as hear the weapons technician below decks, whose image disappeared when the transmission ended.

"Very well. This is a final Fleet Order. Captains, check in."

"*Scarza Val*, target acquired and locked."

"*Nogena*, target acquired and locked."

"*Tiz Velaxa*, target acquired and locked."

"*Morguz Pri*, target acquired and locked."

It took a few more minutes for each of the nearly one hundred ships of the attack fleet to check in and report that their targets, each ship of the Vidarean Navy, had been acquired and a lock had been achieved.

"Admiral," Troka said when the last ship had reported in, "it's done. The fleet stands ready, all targets locked."

"Fleet Order. Disengage all safeties, report failures only."

Only one ship reported in, a Ruudian battle cruiser. "*Roani Pri*, this is the *City of Cavel*. Reporting safety failure."

"Stand down, *City of Cavel*. Transfer target acquisition data to—" She turned to Troka. "Who's the first reserve?"

"*Chaba Naq*," Troka replied.

"*Chaba Naq*, stand by to receive target acquisition data from *City of Cavel*, disengage safeties and report."

"*Chaba Naq*, target acquired and locked, safeties disengaged."

"Very well." Niz turned to Troka. "Well, may God have mercy on our souls."

"And theirs," he replied, nodding in the direction of Vidare.

"Fleet Order," Niz said. "The order is . . . fire and report." With that dry command, the guns of one hundred ships sent highly charged energy blasts in the direction of Vidare, lighting the black ocean ahead of them for miles.

"*Scarza Val*, target indicator dark."

"*Nogena*, target indicator dark."

"*Chaba Naq*, target indicator dark."

Every ship reported success; each target had disappeared.

Niz Elsev felt drained; she could barely talk.

"Contact Admiral Heelvar," she said raspily. "Send out the success code. Then reverse Fleet Order. I'm going below."

*A*T the huge Vidarean naval base in Daribi, aboard one of a hundred ships, a young apprentice seaman turned to his chief petty officer in bewilderment.

"Hey, Chief," said the young seaman, "what the hell's the deal here? Who put out the lights?" The entire naval base was dark, and every ship's power source had been shut down. There was an eerie stillness to the huge base, which usually bustled twenty-four hours a day.

"It's the changeover, yeh dope," the chief replied. "Yeh know, from thought to voice control. Don't you pay attention to what goes on in the world? They'll come on again in a minute. Don't get your b—"

"*Now hear this, now hear this,*" a voice thundered through the entire base. "*Fleet Order . . . General Quarters, General Quarters! All hands, Battle Stations!*"

An explosion of noise and light shattered the base as all ships powered up at once.

"*Now hear this! Fleet Order! Single up all lines for immediate deployment!*"

The order to single up lines was obeyed immediately. It was a traditional order to cast off that hadn't been taken literally in hundreds of years. There were no real "lines" to single up; ships were held in their moorings by powerful energy beams. At the order to single up, the beams were simply shut off.

"Fleet Order," the young seaman exclaimed, squinting in the sudden brightness, "what the—"

"Let's go, kid, get yeh finger out!" shouted the chief.

"But the whole fleet? Shipping out at once? Chief—"

"The grand admiral needs yeh permission? Let's go!"

Admiral Ro Heelvar, the vice admiral of the Gaiusian Navy and the hopeful ruler of a new empire, was taking a nap when his aide awoke him with news of the fleet action.

"Sir," his aide said excitedly, "Admiral Elsav has transmitted the success code!"

"Well, I'll be damned," he replied. "She actually went ahead with it." He sat up and swung his legs off the bed. "Have all division commanders meet me in my ready room," he ordered. "Tell my orderly to bring in my body armor. And some breakfast. I'm suddenly ravenous."

THE first invasion target was Kadhar, the capital city of Lepang, which bordered Gaius to the south. In an Earth war, it would be a foolishly vulnerable target for invaders, easily accessible by land or by sea. There were no natural barriers, such as mountains or broad rivers, between the city of Kadhar and the Gaiusian frontier.

But since the discovery of zero-point energy, which powered virtually everything on Kivlan, there was no real need for strategic placement of cities. The seat of government no longer needed to be a safe distance from its national borders. While Kadhar had often been invaded by transiting armies and navies during Kivlan's warlike periods in history, the discovery of virtually free and plentiful energy had completely superseded the need for wars of expansion. Kadhar, once a bleak, charmless fishing town with little else but blood and despair—and fish—in its history, had in the last three hundred years evolved into a vibrant metropolis. It quickly became the center of the arts and finance in Lepang, and soon was its premier city. The seemingly endless miles of oceanfront property drew new residents from all over the world, but it was the natives who settled there in droves. Children graduated from college and headed there to seek their fortunes. It was a popular honeymoon spot. Business associations fought for hotel space for their conventions. And Lepangians themselves held the city in such high regard that they had moved the seat of government there from Sivay two hundred years before.

The city, as marvelous as it was, was absolutely useless from a military standpoint. It commanded no vital accesses, it boasted no coveted resources, and it opened no significant doors to the rest of the continent. In purely crass terms, all it really had to offer was style and a population that adored it. A smart military commander would simply bypass it. But like Paris in World War II, when that fabled city was conquered, it would take the heart right out of the rest of the country.

And that was what Ro Heelvar was counting on. Besides, he *loved* those oceanfront cafés.

THE city of Kadhar always had a festive air about it, even on ordinary days. The city's motto was "Each day a blessing," and the residents of Kadhar all seemed to believe it. Bright, pastel-colored banners extended from the doorways of almost every building. There always seemed to be musicians and vendors and entertainers on the streets. Even the police, who were renowned for their patience and dry humor as well as their professionalism and good judgment, still wore the same bright, ceremonial (and somewhat uncomfortable) garb they had worn for centuries.

But for Global Feast Day, the city was determined to outdo even itself. There would be parades, concerts, picnics, and balls; there would be art, theater, and sports exhibitions, and some of the greatest stars of those mediums would be giving free performances as gifts to their fellow citizens.

Kadhar was set for the greatest celebration in its history. Managing the hundreds of thousands of people who would participate would take some logistical planning, but no real trouble was expected; a riot along the lines of what had happened in Creves was considered far beneath Kadharian sensibilities.

The mayor of Kadhar, Bohz Remor, was deeply within his element. Remor, a tenth-generation Kadharian, was tiny by Kivlanian standards, but a powerful and charismatic personality, nonetheless. He was the perfect choice for mayor, blessed with a gift of joy that was unmitigated by an equally inherent toughness and resiliency that was both physical and political. He was a one-man band of a person, deeply passionate about his beloved city, and his fellow citizens returned the feeling. He was serving in his fifth term as mayor, and often bragged that his last breath would be in the Mayoral House. Today would be a special day for him and his city; he could feel it. Global Feast Day, he boasted, would be talked about for decades to come.

As it happened, he was absolutely correct.

THE mayor was dressing in his best suit, complete with the orange and lime green sash—the city's colors—that was his ceremonial badge of office, when his aide entered his private quarters.

"Sir? A General Brohn is here to see you. He says it can't wait."

"General Brohn?" he asked as he adjusted the sash. "Never heard of him. Tell him to make an appointment."

"He's the vice-chief of staff, Mr. Mayor. He says it's urgent."

"All right," the mayor sighed. "But it'll have to be quick."

The general, a much older man who had been deservedly nicknamed "the Diplomat," was not in dress uniform but in battle fatigues, which immediately set off warning bells in the mayor's head.

"General? I've got a sick feeling that you're not here for the party."

The mayor was exactly the way he had been described; bright, pugnacious, and impossible to dislike. The general knew immediately that nothing but total frankness would be accepted by this man.

"I'm afraid you're quite right, Mr. Mayor."

"Call me Bohz, General. I served one hitch in the Army—national service—and never got any higher than buck-ass private."

"I'll come straight to the point, Mr. Mayor," the general replied smoothly. "A Gaiusian-Ruudian invasion force is at this very moment massing at the border."

The mayor blinked once. "What?"

"I'm afraid it's true, sir. Apparently, the Gaiusian vice admiral has done a header off the deep end. Another admiral, a Ruudian, is helping him."

"But why? What the hell for?"

"There is no military or political logic to it, sir. It would apear to be no more than an act of vanity."

"What's the prime minister of Gaius doing through all this? Playing with himself in a corner somewhere?"

"He's out of contact, Mr. Mayor. We can only assume that he's under close arrest."

"What about the strike forces themselves? I can't believe they'd stand for this!"

"They have been led to believe that it's an exercise. They don't know that the safeties on their weapons, particularly the artillery, have been disabled."

The mayor was attempting to hold his famous temper. "Well, what the hell can I do about it?"

"Cancel the celebrations," the general said.

The mayor stared in disbelief. "Are you serious? I've got four million people who are just getting out of bed and readying themselves for the biggest day in Kadhar's history. What do I do? Go on the comms and say, 'Uh, folks, sorry, Feast Day is off, we're being invaded for the first time in three hundred and twelve years. Try not to panic, and have a nice day.' "

"I don't know that I'd put it exactly like that, Mr. Mayor, but nevertheless—"

"Lepang Central Command has been informed, have they not?"

"Yes, sir. We are getting ready to move. We're also expecting the Vidarean First and Fifth Light Airborne, and elements of Siga's Third Air Wing—"

The mayor began stripping off his formal attire while scrolling through his closet inventory for his all-but-forgotten battle fatigues.

"General, will you be in command on the ground here?"

"I will be commanding Army Group One of three."

"Then, I will be under your command. I hereby reactivate myself into the Lepang Army Reserve. However, as mayor of Kadhar, my authority supersedes yours for the moment, does it not?"

"Of course it does, sir."

"Then my last order, before you become my commanding officer, is that you do everything you can to keep the fighting away from Kadhar. Force them to bypass it. Is that understood?"

"But, Mayor—how can I promise that?"

"You're an experienced general, damn it, you figure it out!"

"Why don't you warn the city?"

"What good will that do? It'll just cause a panic, and I won't have that. Just keep those Gaiusian bastards out of my city. Clear?"

"Clear, sir," the general sighed.

"That's 'Private' to you. Let's go."

ADMIRAL Meran Topak, who was in temporary charge of the spearhead ground-attack units, was not having as pleasant a morning as Vice Admiral Heelvar. In fact, he wasn't having a pleasant morning at all. Sleep had been virtually impossible the night before, coming only in snatches of several minutes each, and all of them were ended abruptly with visions of his own death.

Meran Topak was having second thoughts.

Although Topak was a bright tactician and an excellent administrator, he really didn't have the creativity or the toughness for supreme command. It was not that he lacked courage, rather it was a want of commitment that brought him up short. Unlike Ro Heelvar or Niz Elsev, who, having made their vital decisions, had long since gotten past them and gone on to do whatever was necessary to make them work, Topak was filled with self-doubt.

It had all seemed such a wonderful idea at first. A walk-over, no resistance, and quick conquest made easy by the vanquished who would so desperately want to avoid spilling even one drop of blood. And who *cared*, really, if the government changed hands? Life on Kivlan wouldn't revert to darkness; there would just be a different guy on top.

But the rumble of field pieces and motorized artillery made his hair stand on end. He suddenly thought of the Global Feast Day celebrations that would occur today, and wished desperately that he was at home with his family, instead of getting ready to ruin the day for everyone. I'm not a bad guy, he thought, why am I behaving like one? Why am I allowing myself to go down in history as one of Kivlan's great villains?

"Admiral, sir?" Topak's aide interrupted his troubled reverie. "Secure from Admiral Elsev."

"Fine. Thank you," he said in polite dismissal.

The image of Niz Elsev appeared sitting opposite him. Topak was surprised to note that she looked as exhausted as he felt.

"Niz!" He attempted heartiness, and even as he spoke, he knew Niz would never buy it. "I heard the success code. Congratulations! I knew you could do it."

Niz did not respond. Instead she just gazed at him steadily.

"Things are going just fine here, Niz. Everything is good to go."

Niz still did not answer.

"Hell of a job there, Niz," he said, his tone becoming a little strained. "But that's what we've come to expect from you."

Niz nodded her head away from him. Her image vanished and was replaced by a giant map of the Vidarean Sea. A vast swarm of light points was headed eastward toward Lepang. The picture then expanded, widening its scope. A second swarm of equally numerous light points followed hard behind.

"Niz?" he gasped. "What is the meaning of this?"

"I think you know," she replied.

"You never were with us, were you, Niz?"

"You can stop this, Meran."

A tear slid down his eye. It surprised him. "No, I can't."

"Then may God have mercy on your soul, Meran."

"I don't think He will," Meran replied. "Good-bye, Niz."

Niz held up a hand to meet Meran's. The two holographic figures made an illusion of touching. Then Niz's figure receded and disappeared.

"Bank of Commerce, Ruud," Meran said.

"Bank of Commerce, hold for identity check. Admiral Topak, how may we be of service?"

"Transfer all accounts and securities to my wife's name."

"Transfer complete, all holdings now in the account of Topak, Bix. Will there be anything else?"

"No, thank you. MedCentral, please."

"Thank you for calling MedCentral. Hold for light sen-

sor. Thank you. There are no adverse conditions at this time."

"I wish to terminate at once."

"Are you sure?"

"Yes."

"Are your affairs in order?"

"Yes."

"Please remain motionless for light sensor. This is your last opportunity to cancel this request. Thank you."

"Proceed at once."

"Remain motionless for light sensor. We're sorry, MedCentral is unable to comply with your request for self-termination at this time. Thank you."

"Why the hell not?"

"Sensors indicate deep emotional stress and trauma. Self-termination has not been given the careful consideration such a decision merits. Our program will not engage assisted self-termination under these conditions. Please take another look at your life and see if you can overcome the problem. Thank you, and have a nice day."

"Well, that's just great," Topak fumed. "Just what in the hell am I supposed to do now?"

CLAUDE Monroe looked out the window of the presidential chamber and up at the night sky.

"The sun will be up in two hours," he said. "I guess things will start moving soon, won't they?"

"Why?" asked Ted Dacos.

Claude looked around, flabbergasted. "Well, it'll be dawn! You know, sunup? As in, most attacks begin at dawn, preferably from the east, so the rising sun will be in the enemy's eyes?"

Ted chuckled and translated for Grig and Dara. "This is *Kivlan*, Major. I suppose that's how you do things on Earth, but here on Kivlan, no one would dream of starting a war before noon at least."

"I don't understand."

"I don't understand why you don't understand. Who can do anything at dawn? Would you have soldiers fight without a good night's sleep? Without a good breakfast? Before the fears and phantoms of a long night have dissipated?"

"I guess it is an entirely different planet."

A communications channel opened, seemingly from nowhere. "Mr. President, the airborne spearhead is ready for departure."

"Just a moment, please." He translated the message for his guests.

"Ooh! Matt!" exclaimed Claude Monroe.

"No way!" Matt retorted.

"Just as an observer, I promise."

"They can't guarantee your safety, Claude. What do I tell your wife? What do I tell your *father-in-law* while he's crushing my spleen? 'Uh, General Hines, I'm really sorry, but they promised me Claude would be perfectly okay.' "

"Oh, don't be such a squid, Matt. Come on, it's research! I'll do a paper on it for the Naval War College: *The Effects of Combat on Alien Cultures*." Claude turned to Grig. "Mr. President, I implore you."

Grig looked appealingly at Matt, who finally shrugged.

"Yes!" Claude shouted. *"Re-con!"*

"Major, please," Ted Dacos winced. "A little restraint." Claude smiled guiltily in response. "We'll fit you with a comm-bank," Ted continued. "It straps on your arm. You'll be able to understand what everyone is saying."

"I'm going, too," Butch Caldwell declared. "Come on, Matt! We can't let this lunatic jarhead go off by himself. Someone has to keep him cool."

"I wash my hands of the two of you," Matt said, giving up. "Excuse my children, Mr. President, they've never known how to behave in public."

TWELVE

ADMIRAL Meran Topak had spent much of the morning trying to work up the nerve to commit suicide.

He hadn't realized it would be so difficult. After all, he had lost his honor—although fortunately, under Kivlanian custom, his family would not be ostracized—his career was over, and he would go down in history as an evil buffoon. Not even the *boss* bad guy; just a stooge. The worst kind of dupe.

He had tried pointing his pistol at various parts of his head and his heart. One simple blast would blow a hole clear through to the other side and he would be dead the split-second after pulling the trigger. So why couldn't he do it? What was preventing him?

Bix?

They used to have such fun together. He used to make her laugh. Everyone had thought she was an ice maiden when they met, coldly beautiful and utterly inaccessible. Yet he'd never given it a thought. The young, newly commissioned officer and the belle of the military ball hit it off from the very first. She had told him that first night that she'd never marry into the military, thank you; that conviction had lasted all of two weeks.

So what had happened to him? Had he changed so much? When did he decide to settle for being *vice*-chief of staff, *deputy* station commander, *assistant* task force commander? And when did everyone *else* decide that that was all he was good for?

Maybe around the time that he decided that making Bix laugh wasn't the most important thing in the world anymore.

His career, always his damned career. And for what? To end up like this. Well, his career was over, if not his life. If Bix would still have him, he'd . . .

"Comm!" he shouted. "Voice ident *now.*"

"Voice ident actuated, Topak, Meran, Admiral Fourth Rank, Imperial Navy of Ruud."

"Comm, Allied order of battle."

"Yes, Admiral. Gaiusian 1st and 3rd Light Armored Divisions; 2nd Gaiusian and 21st Ruudian Infantry Corps; 231st Gaiusian Elite Assault Regiment; Third Gaiusian Supply Division and 87th Trans—"

"Verify weapon status."

"Safeties disengaged, weapons are hot."

Topak inhaled deeply and closed his eyes. "Comm, all safeties on. Chill all weapons."

"Admiral, that is a direct—"

"I know what it is. Just do it!"

"Sir. You are disobeying orders in the face of the enemy. You have violated the Military Code, Article 4, Section 16, sub-paragraph A, which means—"

"Which means *what*?"

"You are guilty of treason, sir."

"Do as I say!"

"Sir. My overides do not permit me to enable the commission of a capital crime—"

"All right!" Topak exploded. "All right." Topak fumed

for a moment. "Comm. Does a state of war exist at the present time between Gaius, Ruud, Velax, and anyone else?"

"No, sir."

"Is there combat occurring anywhere on this planet?"

"No, sir."

"Has there been any sort of declaration of enmity?"

"No, sir."

"Then how could I be committing treason? By your logic, comm, all I am doing is standing down hot weapons during a mancuver. What's treasonous about that?"

"Nothing, sir."

"Then reengage the goddamned safeties!"

"Yes, sir. Safeties reengaged."

"Erase rearming code."

"Rearming code erased."

"Thank you, comm. Now, if you don't mind, I'm just going to sit quietly until they come to get me." He thought that over for a moment. "Or not," he said, getting up quickly.

GRIG Holma turned away dejectedly from the disposition screen. "Well, there you are, Captain," he said to Matt. "Almost two million soldiers facing each other for the biggest battle this planet has ever seen. Barring a miracle, a new dark age is about to descend upon us."

"I wish there was something I could do," Matt replied.

"If one soldier dies . . . just *one* . . . then everything we've worked for these last three hundred years will be meaningless. And it's all my fault."

"Don't say that," said Leva Holma, who had just entered the room. "Don't be so hard on yourself."

"It is my fault, Mother," he said. "Captain Wiener, Major Fournier, Doctor Conger-Levin, this is my mother, Leva Holma. Mom, you already know the vice president and the minister of science."

"Of course." She shook hands warmly with each of the Terrans. "I've been so looking forward to meeting you," she said in perfect English. "Am I speaking your language properly?"

"Oh, wonderfully," replied Jeanne-Marie, thinking, What a class act. She glanced over at Doralee, who had read her mind and nodded to her.

"Do you think you can win?" Matt was saying to Grig.

Grig turned to Matt in disbelief. "Win? What could we possibly take away from this horror that could ever be confused with winning?"

CLAUDE Monroe and Butch Caldwell sat in an airborne transport regarding the other men around them. This was decidedly different from the drops in which Claude had participated as a recon marine.

The aircraft was about as unlike a Marine transport as you could get. Apparently, aerodynamics didn't figure into any aircraft they built on this planet. A flying Greyhound bus would be more interesting to look at and sit in than this tub. But it was blindingly fast. The trip, which was supposed to cover about 1,700 miles, seemed to take only twenty minutes.

The men and women on board were in the normal introspective state of any soldier before a combat drop. But their battle dress, or lack of it, intrigued Claude. They carried sticklike rifles, but that was all. Claude had crabbed his way into his first battle carrying over a hundred pounds of equipment, plus his parachute. These soldiers wore what seemed to be tight chino-type pants, crew-necked shirts, and soft-soled boots. On their heads were brimless kepis, not unlike the sort German soldiers wore in World War I.

"Say, uh, Claude," Butch whispered.

"What?"

"You notice anything strange about this group?"

Claude shrugged. "They seem perfectly normal to me, except for the fact that it's an entirely different *planet* there, Butch."

"That's not what I mean."

"What do you mean?"

"Well, this is an airborne mission, right?"

"Right."

"Well, where're the goddamn *parachutes*?"

"Interesting point," Claude said, a lot more calmly than he felt. "But I'm sure they're way ahead of you on this."

The aircraft slowed to a hover. Without any sort of command or signal, the soldiers stood up as one and began to file toward the rear hatch. One by one, they began to leap from the aircraft.

"What the hell is this, Airborne Lemming Division?" Butch demanded nervously.

"Just do it, champ," Claude said. "It'll be all right."

"Okay . . . but you're out of my will."

Butch closed his eyes and stepped off, but before he could even begin the Lord's Prayer, a powerful force locked on to his body and began to lower him gently to the planet's surface several thousand feet below. His feet touched the ground softly and the force, or whatever it was, suddenly disappeared. Claude joined him a moment later.

"Wow," Butch exclaimed. "It was like a . . . a giant magnet or something! Cool!"

"Aaah, I like the old way better," Claude replied dismissively.

BOHZ Remor, the mayor of Kadhar, instead of being reactivated at his former rank of private, found himself brevetted as a colonel and assigned to the post of aide-de-camp to General Brohn.

It was his job to inspect the forward positions for combat readiness and report back to the general. This suited him just fine. He wanted to be near the front, but didn't want the responsibility of sending anyone to their death. He also knew that once the shooting started, he would be ordered back to headquarters and he would pointedly ignore the order, fighting it out in the trenches with the rest of the grunts. That was where he belonged, temporary colonel or not.

Most of the soldiers up here, at the very front of the front, knew him or knew of him. As mayor of Kadhar, he was one of the most famous men in Lepang, and it did the soldiers good to see a prominent politician hanging it over the edge as they were.

For neither Remor nor the division he was now visiting were kidding themselves. Once the shooting started, this was going to be the hotspot, right here. It was basically a suicide position because the Lepangians were determined not to be the side that began the hostilities. The first shots would have to come from the Gaiusian-Ruudian end of the field.

There was a certain fatalism up here, thought Remor, one that was quite palpable. The troops were neither frightened nor tense, neither angry nor fired up. They were simply calm and professional, busying themselves with last-minute preparations that were neither hurried nor unhurried, and small random acts of generosity that were completely unforced—sharing a ration, automatically giving one's comrade the cloak off one's back, adjusting one another's equipment unasked.

The pure unself-consciousness of it all moved Remor almost to tears. This was where he belonged, he told himself firmly. To die with troops like these . . . what better way was there?

ADMIRAL Ro Heelvar faced the mirror for the last time. Perfect! He stepped through the hatchway and into the command center.

"As you were," he ordered, when the entire room jumped to attention. A hum of activity picked up again as those in the room returned to their tasks.

Today is the day, thought Heelvar. Everything will be different from now on. From this day forward, no one on Kivlan need ever suffer again! Because, from today, this entire planet and everyone who lives here will be under *my* protection!

"Fire control!" he ordered.

"Fire control ready, sir!"

"Fire control." He paused and took a deep breath, visibly moved by the order he was about to give. "Fire control, execute Plan Y. Commence firing!"

"Plan Y executed, sir. Firing . . ." The fire control officer stared at his screen in horror.

"You were saying, Major?"

"Uh . . . uh . . . firing. . . . uh . . ."

"Major, report!"

"Uh, sir . . . nothing happened."

"What?"

The major's turquoise skin deepened several shades. "Nothing happened, sir. It's not responding!"

Heelvar advanced on the major's console. He ran his hand over it several times.

"What in the hell is going on!" He kicked the console to no avail. "Comm!"

"Admiral Heelvar."

"Why was the firing order disobeyed?"

"Safeties are engaged, sir. Weapons are chilled."

"Well, rearm them, damn it! That's an order!"

"That cannot be done, Admiral. The rearming codes have been erased."

"Who the hell did that?"

"I did." The holographic image of Meran Topak, sitting beside the newly rescued Gaiusian prime minister, had suddenly appeared.

"Topak! You . . . buffoon!"

"Better a buffoon than a traitor, Admiral. I couldn't let you do this, Ro. And neither could Niz. The attack on the Vidarean Navy was a fake, staged for your benefit. The entire Vidarean fleet is steaming this way as we speak, just behind Niz's task force."

"Admiral Heelvar," the prime minister said gravely, "you are under arrest. God help you for the chain of beyond-horrific events you almost set in motion. To the Gaiusian-Ruudian attack force: You are ordered to stand down and return home immediately. You have one hour to begin your withdrawal or face the consequences of your actions. Remember, you are unarmed. As for you, Admiral Heelvar—"

But Ro Heelvar was gone.

"**SO** that's it?" Matt Wiener asked.

"Apparently, yes," Ted Dacos replied.

"Not quite," Dara Widh said.

"What do you mean?"

"Admiral Heelvar. Where is he?"

THE object of everyone's concern was at that moment headed straight for Vidare in his private air transport. Admiral Ro Heelvar had been a commander far too long to ever trust one single plan: He always had a backup, even if, as in this case, he was the only one who knew about it. If Plan A fails, go to Plan B. Only a fool would throw all of his eggs into one basket.

No one would be expecting him to go to Vidare; special teams would be combing the Lepangian Peninsula for him, not realizing he was already hundreds of miles away. Not that he blamed them, of course; he would have done the same.

But Plan B, or in this case, Plan Z, might work even better. That idiot Topak's meddling might just have been a blessing in disguise.

THIRTEEN

THERE were sixteen nukes on board the *Forlorn Hope*, which were grouped into four separate firing clusters. As was his privilege, Lieutenant Bob Rodgers had named each of the four after his favorite girlfriends.

As he labored through the night disconnecting the warheads, he wondered if it were only his imagination, or if the nukes really had assumed the personalities of each girl for which they had been named.

Cluster one, or *Linda*, was exactly like the girl for which she had been named—easygoing, generous, and uncomplicated—and the warheads had been removed smoothly and without the slightest difficulty.

Cluster two, *Amy*, was like her namesake, delicate and requiring smooth and gentle handling, but worth the trouble in the end. *Randi*, or cluster three, seemed complicated at first and caused a few problems at the beginning, but once that difficult point was past, it was all smooth sailing.

That left *Sharon*, or cluster four—beautiful but challenging and extraordinarily stubborn. Like her namesake, this cluster simply refused to budge and was giving Bob Rodgers fits. Sharon was the girl he had come closest to marrying, and the only thing that stopped him was a dread fear of bickering constantly for the rest of his life.

"How goes it, Bob?" came John Ryham's voice from the bridge.

"Linda, Amy, and Randi are down, but Sharon is being a royal pain in the butt, bless her heart. Any news?"

"Nothing as yet—wait one. Repair ship coming alongside with docking collar extended. Secure until docking complete."

"Are they back already?"

"I don't—that's odd. There's no communication from the ship at all."

"Maybe they're in trouble! Dock as quick as you can!"

"Right," John replied calmly.

The docking went off with a harder bump than before, but no damage was done. John opened the airlock as soon as the sensors declared it safe to do so.

Ro Heelvar stepped into the *Forlorn Hope*, leveling a blast pistol at John Ryham.

"Bob? Bob, we've got trouble."

Bob's concerned voice came over the intercom. "What kind of trouble?"

"You wouldn't have a weapon on board, would you?"

"Well, I've got a thermonuclear bomb or two, but something tells me that won't quite fit the bill."

"You'd better get up here."

Ro Heelvar had learned only a few words of English, but he knew they'd be the right ones for the task at hand. He pointed to John Ryham.

"You. Fly. Down."

"Down? Down where?"

"Fly!"

"Okay." He muttered, "The first space-jacking in history and it has to happen to me."

Bob Rodgers was out of breath as he reached the bridge. He looked curiously at Ro Heelvar.

"Who the hell are you?" he asked.

"You. Bomb. I say," Heelvar replied.

"Up yours," Bob replied.

Heelvar did not know what "up yours" meant, but he could tell it was uncooperative in tone. He pointed his gun at John Ryham's head. "Bomb."

"Okay, okay. Bomb."

THE celebration in the president's chamber did not last long.

"Mr. President, this is Colonel Vayo in the space monitoring station."

"What's up, Vayo?"

"The Earth ship, sir. It's heading straight for our atmosphere."

"Have you contacted them?" Grig demanded in alarm.

"We tried, sir. There was no response."

"Well, keep trying. No, put it through here. *Forlorn Hope, Forlorn Hope,* this is President Holma, respond please!"

"It's too late, Mr. President."

"Admiral Heelvar! Stop this, Ro!"

"It's your fault, Grig. Your incompetence, your bungling! Leaving the processors off-line even for a day . . . how could you do such a thing? Leaving our people unprotected—it's inexcusable! This is your fault! You brought this on us!"

"I know," Grig replied, knowing it was foolish to argue. "And I'm going to resign."

"What!" demanded Dara Widh in a harsh whisper.

"You're as crazy as he is!" gasped Ted Dacos in an even harsher whisper.

"I'm proud of you, son," Leva Holma said quietly.

"Yes, Ro," Grig continued, "I'm going to resign. But

first, we have to see our way out of this—"

"There's only one way out of this," Heelvar snapped. *"This planet needs someone they can trust! Someone who cares! And that person . . . is me!"*

"Bob! John!" shouted Matt. "Abort! Abort at once!"

"Tell the Earth captain to shut up if he values the lives of his crewmen," snapped Heelvar.

"Oh, God!" Matt wailed in agony.

"Matt! Do it!" shouted John Ryham. *"Don't think, do it!"*

"Matt! No!" cried Jeanne-Marie.

"There's no choice," Matt whispered. A tear slid down his cheek as he looked at Grig Holma and gave him an almost imperceptible nod.

"Colonel Vayo," Grig ordered in a shaky voice, "arm the defense platform. Lock on to the *Forlorn Hope* and fire."

"Aye, sir, platform armed, target acquired and locked. Firing . . . now."

There was a moment of silence, then static, and then an explosion that sent spasms of pain through the ears of all who heard it.

Matt, Jeanne-Marie, and Doralee were hugging each other in an intense outpouring of grief when the commbank exploded into sound.

"Do you think I'm an idiot, Mr. President? Your defense platform is now careening through space in small pieces. I do like these Earth guns!"

The three *Forlorn Hope* officers stared at each other in surprised relief.

"They're alive," Doralee gasped.

"Yes." Matt sobered immediately. "But that madman has our ship and our nukes. If they're in the suborbital communications blackout, we have no way of knowing where they're going to come down."

"We may have to shoot them down after all, Captain," Grig said. After Matt nodded miserably, Grig added, "But we might not be able to. The admiral would know all of the soft grids on the planet."

" 'Soft grids?' " Jeanne-Marie asked.

"I think you would call them"—he whispered to Ted Dacos—"yes, blind spots. We could be quite helpless."

Matt drew himself up with a lot more confidence than he felt. "Don't give up yet, Mr. President. I've got two excellent young officers up there. They aren't about to let this happen without a fight."

Admiral Heelvar was yelling at Bob Rodgers while John Ryham fought to keep the ship's attitude at zero degrees for reentry.

"Hey! Hey, blue boy!" Rodgers shouted at Heelvar. "I don't understand what the hell you're saying! I'm an American! I speak *English*. I also speak German . . . some bootleg Russian . . . and a little French . . . but what I *don't* speak is that . . . pig Latin you're jabbering in!"

"I think he wants you to get ready to drop the bomb," John shouted over his shoulder.

The *Forlorn Hope* shot out of the orbital blackout, hurtling downward with frightening velocity. Ro Heelvar smacked John Ryham's shoulder repeatedly, right and then left, as a crude and violent method of navigation.

Heelvar then made a backward motion with his hand, which John took to mean slow down. He cut back on the throttles as the shoreline of Daribi came into view.

"Wow!" exclaimed Bob Rodgers, who had come up to the bridge for his first close-up view of another planet. "It looks like San Diego!"

"Bombs!" shouted Heelvar.

"All right, all right, don't get your bowels in an up-roar."

Heelvar made another hand motion, this time for John to lower his altitude.

"I can't go any lower without switching off the engines! We're at four thousand already!"

"You! Bomb! I say!" Heelvar shouted at Rodgers.

"I heard you the first time, your voice carries," Bob retorted.

The Executive House came into view. The seal of Vidare was plainly visible on the roof.

"Bomb!" shouted Heelvar.

John looked back at Bob with a pained expression. Bob shrugged helplessly, turned the key, and pressed the lighted red button.

"THE Earth ship has dropped a missile!" Vayo's agitated voice cried. "It's headed straight for . . . for you, Mr. President."

"Oh my God, forgive me," Matt prayed.

Grig Holma felt nothing, just an odd sense of serenity. He put his arm around his mother and the two moved over toward Jeanne-Marie.

"I would have courted you," he said softly. Leva Holma stroked her son's hair.

"I would have liked that," Jeanne-Marie replied.

"Admit it, you were interested," Ted Dacos said to Dara Widh.

"I can say it now," Dara Widh smiled sadly, "I was *very* interested."

"Everyone!" Grig Holma called, spreading out his arms. Everyone immediately joined in a large communal embrace.

"So, we'll all be together in the next world," Grig said.

Matt Wiener finally closed his eyes and whispered, "Ann."

THE small nuclear bomb screamed downward, its little onboard camera providing a blurred view of the ground rushing upward to John, Bob, and Ro Heelvar.

John was literally flying for his life, attempting to get the craft out of the bomb's range, so he hadn't the time to think about the consequences. Ro Heelvar was at peace, looking almost smug. And Bob Rodgers was doing something he hadn't done since the day he left home to enroll at MIT—he was praying.

THE bomb's shriek was highly audible now, as the end of all things came rushing downward. It would be only moments before the bomb impacted on the roof but no one would be able to hear the giant

C
   L
     U
       N
         K
          !

The embrace broke immediately. "Rodgers!" shouted Matt in glee. "You son of a bitch!"

"What happened?" Grig wanted to know.

"He dropped a cold one," Jeanne-Marie said. To his puzzled expression, she replied, "One that couldn't explode."

"We'd better get up to the roof and clean it up," Matt said, taking charge. "And I'll bet there's a hell of a dent up there."

RO Heelvar shrieked in rage.

"Oh, Bob," John called, "I think our friend here needs some first aid."

"Right," Bob's voice came back. He strode up to the bridge and, without stopping to think, ripped the first aid kit out of its casing and conked Ro Heelvar over the head with it. The admiral slid to the floor, unconscious.

"Why in hell didn't we just do that before?" John wondered. "And what happened, thank God?"

Bob shrugged. "Well, I didn't have time to take out the warhead, so I tried to disarm it, but I wasn't quite sure if I had or not."

"You weren't sure?" John's voice went up an octave.

"Hey, man, what can I say? I can just put it down to this: It was *Sharon* all the way. Always kept me guessing, always made me nervous, *always* drove me nuts. But you know what? She never once, ever, about anything, ever let me down."

"Sounds like a marriage made in heaven," John remarked.

Bob grinned. "You never know," he said.

"**THIS** is *Forlorn Hope* calling Vidare, come in please."

"Ted Dacos, *Forlorn Hope*. It's good to hear your voice. Is the admiral all right?"

"This schmuck's an *admiral*?" Bob Rodgers asked, prodding the inert Ro Heelvar with his toe.

"He's not a well man, *Forlorn Hope*. But he was a fine officer."

"This is John Ryham, sir. The admiral is in our custody. Minister, we need to land. We need the longest runway you've got, sir. We are very heavy with fuel."

"Can't they return to orbit?" Ted Dacos asked Matt.

"No way," Matt shook his head. "They'd burn it all up getting back into orbit, then we'd have nothing with which to return home. We may be stuck here for a while." Matt thought of Ann and got a twinge in his chest.

"You left someone behind?" Ted asked him.

Matt patted Ted's shoulder. "Minister, it looks like you and I have something in common. We both have a thing for women in high places."

Ted smiled, not quite understanding, then turned his

attention back to the *Forlorn Hope*. "How long a runway do you need?"

"Eleven, maybe twelve thousand feet," Matt replied.

"And a 'feet' is . . ."

"A foot. One foot, two or more feet." Matt held out his hands approximately twelve inches apart. "See, we usually come in with our tanks empty and deadstick—glide—in without engines. This time, they'll be coming in hot and heavy."

"Hmm. You see, Matt, we haven't used runways for centuries. Oh, well, can they stay aloft for an hour or so on what they've got?"

"I would hope so," Matt replied.

"Good. Well, we'll just have to build you a runway."

THE *Roana Pri*, at the head of the returning task force, finally sighted land.

"Well," Captain Troka Dorig said. "It's over. We did it. *You* did it, Niz."

Niz Elsev nodded wearily. "We all did it. It's good to know that we can fight just as hard to avoid a war as we can to win one. And now if you don't mind, I'd like an air transport to get me home. My husband and kids are waiting."

FOURTEEN

BREVET-COLONEL Bohz Remor, now demobilized and once again simply the mayor of Kadhar, made it his business to take the two Earth soldiers under his wing. He made them his special guests for the celebration of Global Feast Day.

"I love this guy!" Butch Caldwell said. "He's so . . . New York!"

"What does that mean?" Claude Monroe demanded. "I mean, what the hell does that mean? I hear apple-knocking ridge runners like you say that crap all the time, and I still don't what the hell you're talking about. This guy's the mayor of *another city on a different planet,* for God's sake. How can he be 'New York'?"

"Well, he's such a character," Butch said. "I meant it as a compliment," he added weakly.

"I'm sure you did," Claude replied. "And black folk got rhythm and Jews make wonderful accountants. Come on, redneck, let's go party."

Claude Monroe, thinking back to his years as a less

than productive member of society, was amazed at the sight of a beautiful, almost baroquely designed city filled to overflowing with over a million celebrants, and no one seemed to be breaking the law. No one was drunkenly peeing against a building wall. Nowhere in evidence were any pickpockets, muggers, or marauding gangs. Even the police, dressed in finery reminiscent of the Vatican's Swiss Guards, didn't seem to be watching the crowd with any great concern. They were just standing around shooting the breeze like bored cops on a low-hazard detail anywhere in the universe.

"Your city is a showplace," he shouted through his comm-bank at Bohz Remor. "I've never seen anything like it."

"Have a drink," Remor said, taking a glass of Kadharian red wine from a street vendor and handing it to Claude.

Butch reached into his pockets and said, "I'd buy you one but—"

"No one buys anything today," Remor said. "It's Global Feast Day. Come on."

The crowd parted for the mayor, who fielded handshakes and backslaps as he went by. But the sight of the two Earthmen emitted a huge gasp from the crowd. Claude and Butch were slightly afraid for a moment, until they realized that the crowd was welcoming them.

"Mr. Mayor," Claude said. "There's something I need to ask you. Something puzzles me."

"By all means, Major," Remor replied. "What sort of host would I be if I allowed my guests to remain puzzled?"

"Sir, I don't know quite how to put this, but . . . well, we're *aliens*. Beings from another planet. And everyone's being very nice and all, but apart from making us feel as welcome as I guess it's common to do on your world, it doesn't seem like, well, that big a deal to anyone."

"Hmm," Remor gave an interested chortle. "Should it

be? A 'big deal,' as your translator tells me?"

"Quite frankly, sir, yes. On our planet, the landing of extraterrestrials would be all over the media. Everyone would be going nuts. People would be happy, they might be frightened, they might be angry, or they might even think the end of the world has come, but yes, I guarantee you, they would most certainly be *interested*."

Remor put a hamlike mitt on each of the pilots' shoulders. "Is yours a happy world? Are most people glad to be where they are? Or is there suffering, poverty, hatred?"

"Yes," Butch replied. "And I don't see it ever *not* being that way."

"Then it always will be that way," Remor said sadly. "Look, I'm not saying Kivlan is Paradise. We have our problems. There will always be greedy, weak, evil, and sick people. Witness poor Admiral Heelvar. But we've come a long way. Our planet doesn't fear them anymore. We see them and we try to help them. It doesn't always work but . . . I'm getting off the subject.

"We know there's life out there. We weren't surprised that you found us. We're just not, as you said, that interested. Not that you're not welcome; it's just that we don't need a new world. Our history is dark and it's violent and it took us a long time to create a world we all love. I suppose it may be a foreign concept to you, but we're happy. Look at me. This is the city I love. I don't need to be anywhere else."

Claude shook his head in admiration. "You're right, sir. It is a foreign concept."

"All right," Remor said agreeably, "then try this concept. It's just a lot easier to get along. Look at this crowd," he added, sweeping his arm at the huge assemblage. "If someone needs to get through, people make a hole for him. Why? Why not? It's just *easier* than causing a problem."

Remor laughed heartily and patted Claude's shoulder. It occurred to Claude that this was a planet of touchers.

He was struck by something familiar about the way these people acted and he wondered why that was. Then a thought struck him: He was reminded of his uncle-in-law, former detective, now deputy inspector, Frank Hines. Frank had a way of dealing with suspects—and people in general from whom he wanted information. It was a sort of verbal judo—in the literal sense, as judo was Japanese for *gentle way*—in which he never argued, never threatened, but was always accommodating. He had seemed to Claude, back when they were adversaries, to come across as more like a soft salesman than a cop, which was why Claude, as bright as he was, had always underestimated him. When Frank was on a field interrogation, he treated everyone as though they were not only important but a celebrity or even a relative. He always made sure they were comfortable and relaxed, even took the time to find something, anything, about the person to compliment, even to the point of awe. And later, when they had become family and Claude asked him about it, he had given him the same answer as Mayor Remor: "It's *easier*." That was one reason why Frank was able to close more cases than anyone who had ever worked Brooklyn South, the precinct he now commanded.

The difference was that Frank acted that way to get what he needed from someone. Here on Kivlan, they including and especially the mayor, acted that way because that was their nature.

They followed the mayor up to a huge platform, where he stood and raised his hands for silence. There was still too much noise, so they could not hear through their translators exactly what was being said, but Remor was gesturing toward them and eliciting much applause for doing so.

There was another gasp from the crowd, and the front of every building surrounding the square became a sort of giant projection screen. Everywhere Butch and Claude looked, they could see the *Forlorn Hope* silhouetted against the cloudless azure sky, flared for landing.

It seemed as though they were going to land on the water going straight into Daribi Marina, but that was where Ted Dacos had had a twelve-thousand-foot runway hastily constructed.

Both pilots watched carefully. "Come on, John," Butch urged quietly, "grease it on in!"

"Keep the nose up, John," Claude thought aloud.

But they needn't have worried. John Ryham had not finished at the top of every RAF training class for nothing. The spacecraft touched down with barely a thump, and John quickly reversed thrust and coasted to a smooth stop like a chauffeured Rolls to a traffic light.

The crowd roared its appreciation. "Way to go, John!" shouted Butch.

"Oh, my God!" Claude Monroe cried suddenly.

"What?"

"If the *Forlorn Hope* is down here . . . how are we gonna get home?"

THE unconscious Ro Heelvar was taken away by MedCentral technicians as John Ryham and Bob Rodgers were greeted by their relieved captain. Both were glad to be off the ship and out in the fresh air and sunshine after being cooped up for months, but worry set in immediately.

"What are we going to do, Matt?" John Ryham asked. "We're stuck here."

"Right now, let's just relax and get our bearings."

"Where're Butch and Claude?" Bob asked, as he fielded kisses from Jeanne-Marie and Doralee.

"They're in Lepang. They'll be back tonight."

"What's Lepang?"

"The Paris of this planet, from what I've been told."

"Ooh-la-la. Do we get to stay at a hotel or something? I need a nap big-time. And a shower would be nice."

"It's all taken care of. And our presence is requested at the Gin-cha tonight."

"What's a Gin-cha?"

"I guess we'll find out."

The Gin-cha, not to put too fine a point on it, was the damnedest place any of the crew of the *Forlorn Hope* had ever imagined. When Matt had asked the president exactly what the Gin-cha was, Grig Holma had replied, "Anything you want it to be." Matt had considered that a rather ambiguous reply to a simple and direct question, but because he already felt that he knew the president well enough not to expect rudeness, he began to wonder what Grig meant. Matt would soon find out; the president meant exactly what he said.

The Gin-cha, as Ted Dacos had originally told them, was a nightclub. People went there to dance, and the music was quite audible outside even and a block away. What shocked Matt and—as evidenced by quick eye contact—he others of the crew, was how *bad* the music was. It wasn't even bad, really; it was simply very uninspired, like the score of a cheap 1970s porno movie. Apparently Kivlan wasn't centuries ahead of Earth in *everything*.

But everyone seemed to like it well enough to dance to it. The locals, as the crew began referring to Kivlanians, were moving to the beat, dancing not particularly well but with obvious enjoyment.

All ten of them—including Ted Dacos and Dara Widh, and Butch and Claude just in from Lepang—had walked the few blocks from Executive House to the Gin-cha. That in itself had flabbergasted the crew of the *Forlorn Hope*; the president, simply walking to a neighborhood club— no security, no advance people, no press, no anything. And everyone left him alone, like a movie star who had become a familiar fixture in his own neighborhood. Matt tried to imagine Ann doing the same thing—impossible, even in his own mind. Such a visit would have been planned weeks in advance, security in place days before, traffic redirected blocks away, no one allowed anywhere near the place without passing through a Secret Service gauntlet. And yet all Grig had said was, "Everyone's here to have a good time, not to bother me."

The Gin-cha was crowded and loud and, amazingly, blank. It was a cavernous garagelike structure with seemingly no atmosphere at all. There were ten small island-type bars dispersed throughout the room, but that was all. The crew of the *Forlorn Hope* were wondering what all the fuss was about this desolate, giant hole-in-the-wall when an attractive woman in a sleek leotard bodysuit approached the president, bowed, and handed him an object that looked like an oversized Christmas tree ornament.

Grig Holma bowed gallantly and handed the ball to Jeanne-Marie. "Anywhere you want it to be," he said. "Think of your favorite club in the world—your world."

"This ball can do that?" she asked.

"Try it and see. Just hold the ball in your hands and think of the place that makes you happiest."

She closed her eyes and only momentarily thought of Orbegozo's on Martinique. But that was all it took. A warm and moist salt breeze filled her nostrils and she opened her eyes quickly. The empty room had vanished, and she and everyone else were now at the open beach club right on the Caribbean. She could hear, and even see, the waves lapping against the shore. There were thatched-roofed bars, and the floor beneath her was now sandy beach.

"Major Fournier! The world's most beautiful test pilot! Welcome back, *ma chèri* Jeanne-Marie!"

"Laurent? Is that you, Laurent? What are you doing here?"

"Where else would I be?" the ebullient little firebrand who owned the nightspot asked her.

"Is this true?" she asked Grig.

"The ball takes the best part of your memories. Your

friend is quite real, I assure you, as real as your memory can make him."

"Laurent, this is my friend Grig Holma, the president of the nation of Vidare on the planet Kivlan."

Laurent came to attention at once. "Monsieur le President," he said gravely. "Anything you desire, anything at all. You and *la commandante* are my special guests." He bowed, kissed Jeanne-Marie's hand, and whisked off.

Jeanne looked around her. The Kivlanians in the room, or on the beach, such as it was, seemed to be enjoying the place immensely. In fact, seemingly as one, all of the Kivlanians looked over at her and began beating their fingertips on their tables. This was a memory that the ball would be called upon to conjure long after the *Forlorn Hope* had left to go home.

"That means they approve," Grig responded to her puzzled expression. "Shall we dance?"

"The 'courting' you spoke of before?" she asked slyly.

"Yes." Grig couldn't understand it, but here was this heart-stoppingly beautiful woman and she seemed to like him! She didn't care that he was big and fat, that he obviously was inexperienced, that they came from different worlds. She somehow saw through all that and he somehow knew it. What a night!

The locals in the crowd also sampled the delights of the Elephant Bar when it was Claude's turn, the St. Regis bar during Matt's, and the Mutiny in Miami when Doralee was given the ball.

It was during John Ryham's turn that the talk turned serious between Grig and Matt. John Ryham had initially refused the ball, saying that the present atmosphere— Rolly's in New Orleans—was fine with him.

"I understand," he said to Grig Holma, "that you are a planet of pipers."

"Yes," Grig replied in surprise. Jeanne-Marie's head was on his shoulder, and he hadn't a clue that the evening could improve at all. "Do you play?" he asked incredulously.

"I'm a Scotsman," John shrugged, "or half of one, anyway."

Grig Holma called over a waiter and told him to bring a bagpipe. The waiter complied instantly, even though he was an imaginary server from the recesses of Butch Caldwell's memory.

John picked up the strange-looking pipes. They were not wood but instead a sort of metallic-polymer blend, and there was no tartan sash extending downward. But an exploratory breath or two assured him that these pipes were not too different than the ones he had grown up playing.

"I didn't know you played the pipes, John," Doralee said.

"I was a lonely fat kid," John replied. "Is there a more accurate musical expression of loneliness than the bagpipe?"

Grig Holma felt John's careless words like a kidney punch. A flash of anger swelled within him and disappeared just as quickly as it came. He looked over at John with a new sense of comradeship that reached far across the galaxies. Some things were universal, after all.

"Play for us, John," he said with a catch in his throat. "Take the ball."

John held the ball for only a moment and the loud smoky New Orleans jazz club vanished without leaving even an echo hanging in the air.

The room let out a collective breath as they drank in their new surroundings—a lonely, misty, green Scottish Highland moor.

John stood up, and the crowd in the room—or out on the moor—seeing that bagpipes were present, quieted as though for a national anthem.

John launched into "Scotland the Brave." He was soon joined by one hundred other pipers in centuries-old kilts, piping the same tune from far in the distance. The beautiful, haunting melody cut to the heart of everyone present. The applause when he finished was intense and heartfelt and not without tears.

"I've been meaning to ask you, Grig," Matt said, after John began a tune with a bit more lilt to it, "we haven't spoken about getting home. Can you find us a fuel source?"

"I have people looking into it now," he replied curtly. Actually, it was a problem he did not want to discuss without deeper thought. The ship, as he had discussed with Ted Dacos, could easily be refitted for zero-point energy. But that wasn't the issue. The issue was, Did he want to give this technology to a planet that might not be ready for it?

He looked over at the dance floor, where Ted Dacos and Dara Widh had spent much of the night together. He was glad that the two of them seemed to be getting along. But his good mood was only momentary; for the first time in his life, duplicity had been forced upon him. He couldn't just gas up the *Forlorn Hope* with zero-point energy and send them on their merry way. Who knew what sort of whirlwind that might reap?

And there was Jeanne. His first date in a long time. All right, his first date *ever*. And it wasn't going to last, he knew that well. Either she would leave him to return to Earth, or she would find out that he was keeping them all here and hate him. Damn it all! What was he going to do? He looked at Jeanne-Marie, who was talking to Ted Dacos, and realized that she was holding his hand—and had been for some time.

What was he going to do?

A Kivlanian had taken the ball and turned the place into a rather pedestrian-looking dance hall, with the usual bright pastels that so dominated the planet. But the dance was a slow one, and Grig, with Jeanne-Marie in his arms, barely moved at all.

Jeanne-Marie suddenly pushed away from him.

"What's wrong?" he asked.

"Aaah!" She began scratching herself intensely.

"Jeanne! What is it? What did I—"

"Don't touch me!" She backed away. "I feel . . . I . . ." Her eyes rolled back and she dropped to the floor before he could catch her.

"MedCentral!" Grig shouted. The music stopped and everyone gathered around in concern.

"This is MedCentral. Please stand by for light sensor. Thank you. MedCentral advises that the subject now under diagnostic examination is not of normal Kivlanian cell structure. The differences are slight. However, Medcentral does require a release from liability before continuing diagnosis."

"All right, you're released! Now get on with it!"

"Thank you. Please stand by for light sensor. Subject has been critically affected by fallout rash. The subject's constitution makes her more vulnerable to fallout than the average Kivlanian. It cannot be determined just how ill this subject will become. However, MedCentral recommends that she be removed to a self-contained environment as soon as possible. We also suggest that any other subjects of similar constitution be isolated as well."

"MedCentral," Grig said, "We have six others of like constitutional makeup. Dispatch technicians immediately."

"ETA of MedCentral technicians, three point seven minutes. Please keep subjects as calm as possible. Thank you for calling MedCentral, and have a lovely evening."

Grig looked around for the rest of the crew of the *Forlorn Hope.* Five of them were unconscious, with worried Kivlanians hovering over them. The sixth, Matt Wiener, had fallen to his knees and looked at Grig with a puzzled, almost hurt expression that Grig was sure he would see every time he closed his eyes from then on.

Then Matt fell on his hands and joined his crew in oblivion.

FIFTEEN

THE crew of the *Forlorn Hope* had been quarantined in the infirmary of Executive House. As they were taken away from the Gin-cha in medical transports, Grig could not help but sense the deep concern of everyone in the club. These Earth people had, in the short time of their visit so far, become dear to everyone they had met. Even from faraway Lepang, Mayor Remor had reported that the two aliens had mixed in with the crowds so well that it took them an hour just to say good-bye to all their new friends as they boarded their transport to Daribi. And that, to Grig, was the one thing about this whole extraterrestrial visit that utterly amazed him.

He had always known there were others somewhere out in space. And he knew, eventually, they would find their way to Kivlan. But none of that had gone off as he had expected. He had always believed, when he thought about it at all, that when aliens arrived, the meeting would be warm and touching, but with a certain formal distance. There would be ceremony, and study, and a kind of tacitly agreed, slowly forming alliance. But Grig had never thought it would become *personal*. He had never expected that they would simply *hit it off*; that he would meet seven people who would just enter his life, fit right in, and become his friends. Although their acquaintance was short— and forgetting about his intense attraction to Jeanne-Marie—he could no longer imagine his life without these people in it.

How had this happened? They were from a planet so far behind Kivlan, with so many flaws and such a long way to go, and yet these people, this crew, had a quality that was almost Kivlanian. Grig was intelligent enough to realize that, of course, these seven would have to be their best and their brightest, but nevertheless . . . didn't it speak well for the Earth that they had such people at all?

Hadn't he himself fallen in love with one of them?

Grig was pacing the infirmary hall with Dara Widh and Ted Dacos. "I don't understand it," Dara was saying. "Why did the fallout rash hit them so hard? Why were none of us affected?"

"Oh, that's easy," Ted said dismissively. "We Kivlanians have reached critical mass, just as with any plague or virus. Everyone who was ever going to be struck, has been struck. The rest of us, well, we'd've been hit by now if we were going to be. But our Earth friends, they've no immunity built up as we do. And their bodies' immune systems must have been powerless to fight it at all."

A doctor came out into the hall. "Mr. President?"

"Yes, Doctor."

"Sir. I'm happy to report that we have been able to treat the effects of the fallout so far. But . . ."

"But what?"

"If they are exposed to the fallout again, at all, it'll be much worse. Their physical and chemical makeup is not far different from ours, but it is markedly weaker. And this quarantine—it won't work for too much longer."

"Why not?"

"I know why," Ted said. "There is nothing truly self-contained—*hermetically* self-contained—on this entire planet. The eruptions still have another forty or so days to go. That's far too long."

"So, what are we saying here?" Grig demanded.

The doctor stared levelly at the president. "What I'm saying, sir, is get them back into their ship and off this planet."

"Off the planet? Or else what follows?"

"They die, sir. It's as simple as that. And as tough as that."

WHEN Grig Holma was especially troubled, and far too nervous for the bagpipe to soothe him, he went up on the roof of Executive House and stared out at the harbor lights.

Sometimes it worked, and sometimes it didn't. Right now, it didn't.

"What in God's name are we going to do?" he asked Ted and Dara.

"If we don't get them back on their ship and out of here, they'll die," Dara replied. "You heard the doctor."

"Yes. I heard the doctor," Grig said miserably. "But I also heard what Matt said. They don't have enough fuel. He told me that it would take ninety-five percent of their fuel supply just to get them out of orbit. What remains after that won't even get them clear of our galaxy."

"So, can't we give them more fuel?" Ted asked. "We can take a sample out of the tank and manufacture it, can't we? Liquid oxygen, Matt called it. How hard can that be?"

Grig threw up his hands and paced the roof. The night was getting chilly, but he didn't care. He turned back to Ted. "Even if we did, where the hell would we put it? The ship, from what he told me, is attached to these gigantic tanks when it first blasts off. All that fuel gets used up, and once they're out of orbit, they drop the tanks and go on their own power. We don't know anything about that! We could wind up blowing the damn thing to smithereens!"

"There's no choice here, Grig," Dara said quietly. "We'll have to reconfigure their fuel system for zero-point energy."

"You think I haven't thought of that! Hey, they're wonderful people. I love 'em, I really do. But you know what their planet's like. Do we really want to give them the basis of our entire civilization maybe centuries before they're even ready for it? It could be like giving a kid a blast pistol!"

"If we don't do something, they'll die," Ted said flatly. "I don't see what else we can do. We'll just have to take that chance."

Grig shivered and huddled deeper into his tunic. "All right. Just say, for the sake of argument, that I do what you're both suggesting. Who drives the damned ship? None of the crew can; we don't know when they'll recover enough to take over. I can't. I'm not a pilot. I couldn't even drive a transport without thought control. And I won't send one of our own Air Force guys—who knows what kind of danger might be waiting for him or her out there?"

"I'm a pilot," Dara said quickly. "I'll do it."

"No way, Dara. This government cannot spare you. I told you before, I'm resigning. No matter what happens, you are going to be the next president as soon as this crisis is over."

"Grig! How can—"

"Look, I screwed up! I let this planet come dangerously close to war because of my own naiveté. I don't deserve to be president anymore. Besides, twelve years is long enough. But you, Dara, you will be a great president." Grig thought for a moment. "All right. I'll do it. Dara, get the commanding general for Air Force training as soon as possible. He's got to teach me to fly and he has to do it fast. I want—"

"Excuse me, am I interrupting?"

"Mom!"

Leva Holma gathered her shawl about her tightly. "My, the night's turned cold, hasn't it?"

Grig Holma took his mother's hands. "Mom, what brings you up here?"

"Son, you know that I would never interfere with the way that you discharge the duties of your office. I think you've been a wonderful president, and so does the rest of the world."

"Hear, hear," Dara Widh said.

"But," Leva continued, "I also understand why you feel you should resign. If that's how you truly feel, then follow your heart. And you're right; with Dara, the country would be in most capable hands. But, my son, there is one thing you'll never do, and that is *fly*."

"Gee, Ma, thanks for the vote of confidence," Grig said. "This is my mother, folks," he added to the world at large.

"Grig," she said firmly, "flying isn't something that you just *do*. Dara will bear me out on this. You're just like your dear father; strong and brave and brilliant, but useless around anything mechanical. Well, that's flying. You must have a passion for it. And, more importantly, you must have respect for it. You have neither, and you certainly won't achieve it in a matter of *days*."

Grig raised his eyes skyward. "Then you tell me, Ma. What do we do? Who's qualified that can fly that damned thing?"

"Language," she warned him as always. "Why, that's simple," she replied. "I will."

"What!"

"Grig . . . son . . . I'm an engineer. A good one, I like to think. While you were off gallivanting at the Gin-cha, I was studying the ship, reading the manuals. Did you forget that I was a pilot, as well?"

"Yeah, but Ma . . . that was a long time ago and it was Air Force trainers and—"

"Son, there's nothing complicated about the . . . *Forlorn Hope*, I believe it is called? Where did they get that name, anyway?"

"Major Monroe explained it to me," Ted said. "It's from another language of theirs, yes, it's called 'Dutch.' From the words *verloren hoop*, meaning 'lost troop.' But it's also a vanguard, a small group sent forward to take and hold ground."

"Hmm! Interesting. Thank you, Minister. Anyway, son, if I can fly an Air Force trainer, I can certainly fly the *Forlorn Hope*. Besides, I want to see Earth! Give an old woman a thrill, why don't you?"

"Oh, Mom! You're not 'old.' What do you guys think?"

"I say go," Ted replied promptly.

"I think that entire planet is going to fall in love with the both of you," Dara said.

THERE was a lot of work to be done before the *Forlorn Hope* was once again ready to be launched. Not only did the fuel cells have to be reconfigured for zero-point energy, which was a relatively simple task for minds like that of Ted Dacos, but the outer tiles had to be reinforced. The ship would now go much faster than ever before, and the entire structure needed to be strengthened.

A new air supply had to be laid in, and it had to be completely sanitized. DNA samples were taken from the skin scrapings of each crew member, so that medical teams would have a better understanding of the Earth's atmosphere. This would also enable them to create inoculations that would protect Grig and Leva Holma from any Earth diseases or viruses that might invade their systems.

The navigational systems had to be decoded, so that they could find the straightest course back to Earth.

Grig had prepared a communications package of his own, a comprehensive omnibus of Kivlanian history, languages, and a simple tour of everyday life on his planet, including its culture, mores, and technology. There were also greetings from the heads of government of every nation on Kivlan.

Finally, all was in readiness. In a quiet, informal ceremony, attended by few people and no media, Grig Holma passed the reins of government to Dara Widh. She would serve out the remaining year and seven months of his term, but was far from deciding whether she would seek one of her own.

The still-unconscious crew of the *Forlorn Hope* had been carried on board by MedCentral technicians and secured into their own sleeping bays. As Leva Holma completed the preflight checklist, Grig stood out on the runway that had been built for the *Forlorn Hope*'s emergency landing, saying his good-byes to Dara Widh and Ted Dacos.

"Well, I guess this is it," Grig said, embarrassed at the tear that had escaped his eye and ran unchecked.

"We'll miss you, sir," Ted said.

"Me and my mom . . . star voyagers," Grig remarked, with a trace of irony. "Could you ever have imagined such a thing?"

"I always knew you could do anything, Grig," Dara said. "I just wish you hadn't left it all on me."

"You'll be a shining light in Vidare's history, Madame President," Grig said. "That is one decision I know I'll never regret. Now, c'mere, D."

He enveloped Dara in a giant bear hug and kissed her on each cheek. "I love you, D. I know you'll make us all proud." He turned to Ted and embraced him as well. "Vidare needs you more than ever. I know you won't let me down."

"I won't, Mr. President. Grig."

"I guess it's 'ambassador' now, isn't it? Well, I'm off

to Earth. I'll be back . . . God knows when."

He shot them a wink and ran up the gangway.

"**HOW'RE** we doing, Ma? I mean, Captain?"

Leva Holma pushed a button and the hatch sealed shut with a thud and a hiss. "Everything secure, son. That is, everything except you. Will you please sit down, right here beside me, and strap in?"

"Whatever you say, Ma." He looked over at his mother in wonder. There was a light in her eyes he had never seen before, and she looked years younger and really quite beautiful.

"Starting one," she said firmly. "Well, here's where we find out if our energy-source conversion actually worked."

She pressed the starter on the number one engine . . . and it turned over without a second's hesitation.

"Starting two . . ." The result was the same. In a moment, the idling thrust of all eight engines had her feet straining against the toe brakes as if she were holding back a deluge.

"We're ready, son. Are you?"

"Yes, Mom."

"And you're sure you want to do this?"

"Mother, this is what I do."

She smiled. "Fine. Now you be a good boy, or I'm going to turn this ship right around—"

His laughter cut her off. "Stop it, Ma. Let's go to Earth."

"All right." There was a loud whining sound that increased in almost geometric intensity as she brought the throttles forward to the wall. Then she released the toe brakes, and they shot forward into history.

DARA and Ted watched intently as the *Forlorn Hope* sped down the runway, lifted smoothly into the air, and was soon a speck in the far distance.

"They'll be all right," Ted said.

"I know they will," Dara said. "The question is, will we?" She turned and looked into Ted's eyes. "I'm going to need you, Ted."

Ted had never seen that look from her before, which made him heed his own instinct and dismiss the idea of a flip answer.

"You know that I am at your disposal, Madame President."

"My best friend is up there," she said, pointing at the sky. "I need another best friend." She took his hand. "I need an even better friend."

"As I told you, Dara," he said, looking down at her hand clasped in his own, "I am at your disposal. For *everything*."

"**ARE** we in space yet?" Grig asked.

"You see those eight switches with a little bar across them, Grig?"

"Yes, Ma."

"Those are the boosters. That bar is there so you can throw them all on at exactly the same time. I'm going to need both hands on the controls, so you'll have to flip the boosters for me."

"You mean this one down here—" He switched on the boosters and was thrown back in his seat with such violence that it almost made him look around for someone to hit.

"Next time, wait until I tell you," his mother scolded.

"Look! It's nighttime! Stars everywhere!"

"You're in space, son."

"Whooaaaaa! Mom! I feel like I'm turning upside down!"

"You are. We're in a roll maneuver."

"Agghhh, God, I'm gonna heave!"

"No, you won't. Settle back. I'm turning on the Gravitron. This switch here . . . there! Better?"

"I feel like I just sat on my own chest, but at least I'm not sick anymore."

"It's all right, son," she said, shutting down the boosters. "That was the hard part. Now why don't you go check on the others?"

"I can get up now?"

"Of course."

He unstrapped and was about to climb out of his chair when he looked over at his mother, whose confident eyes were scanning the readouts, and whose sure hands were deftly adjusting various controls. For the first time, he saw her not as his mother, but as he now knew everyone else saw her.

"I never told you this before, Ma," he said, with a choked admiration, "but you are . . . terrific."

She reached over and stroked his hair. "You're a wonderful son." She smiled and laughed softly. "Now, go check on the others."

"Okay, Mom. After all, you're the captain."

"Only until Matt wakes up."

Grig started to move back to the crew section of the ship when he stopped suddenly and turned back.

"Mom?"

"Yes, son."

"We're really doing this, aren't we?"

"I would say so."

"I hope I don't screw up. I hope I *haven't* screwed up."

Leva turned around to face her son. "Grig, all I have ever asked you to do was to follow your heart. Whenever you've done that, you've never been wrong."

MATT Wiener's eyes flickered open and he awoke with a shudder. The last thing he remembered was passing out on the floor of that crazy disco. He looked around and

saw that he was in own rack in his tiny compartment
aboard the *Forlorn Hope*. How the hell did that happen?

He reached over and slid open the door to his compartment and saw that all the other cubicle doors were still shut.
He rose up, felt a dizzy spell coming on, and lay back down
again. Then he took a deep breath and gave it another try.
He swung his legs off the rack and put his feet on the floor,
a sheet of ice even through his crew socks.

Matt got up slowly, carefully, and ventured out into the
crew room. He thought he saw Grig Holma seated at the
wardroom table, but he wasn't sure he could believe it.

"Grig? Is that you, Mr. President?"

Grig jumped up at once and took Matt's elbow, helping
him into a seat. "You'd better take it easy, Matt. You've
been out for a few days."

"What the hell happened? Are we in space? Who's flying the ship?"

"My mother. It's fine—"

"Your *mother*?"

Grig pointed to the navigational chart on the wardroom
wall. "I'd say she's doing all right, wouldn't you?"

"Yeah, but what—"

"The fallout rash, Matt. It would have killed all of you.
We had to get you off Kivlan as soon as we could."

"But you're . . . the president. How could you just—"

"I've resigned. Dara's taken over, and she was born to
be president, a far better one than I could ever be. The
important thing was to get you home safely."

Matt stared at the wall, touched. This was beyond any
treaty, beyond any alliance. This was . . . friendship.
"Grig? You say we've been out just a few days?"

"That's right."

"Well, looking at this chart, we're *weeks* ahead of
where we should be! Did you—you did, didn't you?"

Grig shrugged. "You yourself said you'd barely get out
of orbit with the fuel you had on board. We had to get

you off Kivlan . . . there was nothing else we could do."

Matt shook his head in wonder. "When we land, this ship is gonna need tighter security than an A-list movie star."

"A what?"

"Oh, it's an—" He was interrupted by the sound of a cubicle door sliding open. In another moment, Jeanne-Marie Fournier came teetering unsteadily out of her compartment, eyes barely open. On her feet were a silly pair of bunny slippers that a niece had given her as a bon voyage present.

Grig's heart leaped at seeing her again. Even disheveled and barely conscious, she made him tremble. Grig noticed that Matt was watching her with a wry smile across his lips.

"Jeanne is definitely not a morning person," he whispered to Grig. "You could shoot off a cannon in her ears, collapse a building around her, but she's completely in her own world until her first cup of coffee."

Jeanne staggered her way over to them, her eyes barely slits. She stopped at Grig, put a hand on his shoulder, and sleepily kissed him on the lips.

"Morning, sweetheart," she said. Then she clumped around the pleasantly baffled ex-president and over to the coffeepot. She picked up her own personal mug (*Je heart Paris*) and began pouring herself a cup.

Matt nudged Grig on his upper arm. "Watch," he said, unable to keep a straight face, "three . . . two . . . one." He pointed at Jeanne-Marie's back as if to cue her.

"What am I doing here?" Jeanne-Marie asked, still facing away from them.

"Sit down, drink your coffee, and all will be revealed," Matt said. His smile suddenly froze. They were on their way home now, and with the Kivlanian energy source, they'd get there much sooner than ever imagined. And the *Forlorn Hope* would cease to be a crew, a close-knit group of people who loved, respected, and depended upon each other, who knew and indulged each other's quirks and personality traits. Such as Jeanne-Marie first thing in the morning. He would miss them all.

He shook it off. He would also be returning to Ann— if she was still interested after all these months. He shook that off, too. No use thinking about it now.

Jeanne sat down next to Grig. She looked over at him, put her hand on top of his, and began to drink her first cup of coffee on the voyage home.

A few weeks later, Matt was seated at the command console with Leva Holma to his right.

"Well, we're almost there, Mom," Matt said. Leva Holma had become surrogate den mother to the entire crew, who meant every bit of it when they called her mom. "Thanks to your Kivlanian fuel source, a hell of a lot earlier than anyone would ever expect."

"Language," she said with a smile. "I can hardly wait," she said. "Your world sounds so exciting!"

"They are going to absolutely adore you," Matt said. "And I, personally, can't wait to see you after your daughter-in-law takes you shopping in Paris."

"I always knew Grig would find a nice girl," she said. "And he did, he really did."

"I don't know how legal the ceremony really was," Grig said. "In my world, a ship's captain, okay. But a *space*ship captain? I think we really pushed the edge of the legal envelope there. Oh! You see that? Up ahead. That is the most romantic pile of rock in the history of the universe. That's our moon. It's much prettier from Earth."

"Like a lot of old things," Leva grinned. "Better looking the farther away you are."

"Not you, Mom. You may be one hundred and twenty-eight on Kivlan, but on Earth, you are one, hot, swinging sixty, I'd say. The men just aren't going to leave you alone."

"Flatterer."

"Yes, but not an idle one." There was a beep from the communciations console. They were now within voice range of Earth.

"Houston, Houston, this is *Forlorn Hope*, come in Houston."

Matt heard a "What the hell?" and called again. "Hello, Houston, are you conscious down there? This is *Forlorn Hope*, how are you reading us?"

"Whoever you are, this is a violation of a secure government channel. I suggest you—"

"Alex? Alex Rayne? Is that you? Matt Wiener here."

"Matt! What's going on? You're four months ahead of schedule! Is everything all right?"

Matt smiled at Leva. "Houston, we definitely do *not* have a problem. Houston, like the old song says, we are somewhere between the moon and New York City. I'd give our ETA at about thirty-nine hours."

"Admiral, is everything all right?"

"It's better than all right. Be advised, we have two ETs on board, check that, two friends, check *that*, two *dear* friends on board. We will require Level Quintuple-A security for the *Forlorn Hope* upon landing—trust me on this. And our guests rate twenty-one guns and a 'Hail to the Chief.' "

"You brought back an a—"

"Hey, Alex. Did you just call me 'admiral'?"

"The All-Navy List was published last month. Congratulations, Admiral. And you can tell the crew they've all been bumped up a notch as well, even the foreigners."

"Mom, I made admiral," Matt said to Leva. "I never thought it'd be such a big deal, but now . . ."

Leva leaned over the console and kissed Matt's cheek. "I'm so happy I was here when you found out."

"Matt," Alex Rayne called. "One other thing. Personal

from the president. She wants to know, quote, 'Is there still snow on top of Big Bear?' unquote. Matt? Did you get that? Do you have a reply?"

Matt looked over at Leva, his smile wide. "Making admiral? Nothing, next to *this*."

"NO, Prime Minister," President Ann Catesby was telling a Balkan official over a video conference, "the United States has gone out of the police-action business. If this is an official request for military assistance, then understand exactly the assistance you are going to get. I am not going to put American troops in the way of rocks and bottles from children and grenade launchers and machine gun ambushes from alleyways. You have a war to win, and we decide it's a just war, we'll help you win it. *Our way*. Is that understood? Good. Think about it, and then get back to me with a formal request—*if* it's really necessary."

She rang off and her phone buzzed immediately. "What!"

"Sorry, ma'am. Alex Rayne of NASA is on the line. The *Forlorn Hope* is back. They're about halfway from the moon—"

"Alex! They're back? They're four months early! Is everything okay?"

"Ma'am, they're fine. Everything's wonderful, according to their reports. They've also brought some guests—"

Which would have been the news of the century to any other president, and even Ann would allow it to sink in later. But at the moment . . .

"Ma'am, Admiral Wiener has a message in response to your query."

Her heart quivered. "And that is?" she asked, struggling to remain calm.

"Ma'am, the admiral's response, and please take it in

context, is 'There's so much goddamned snow, I can't believe it's even summer . . .' Ma'am? Ms. President, are you—"

"Irv!"

The head of the White House Secret Service detail burst in immediately. "Ms. President?"

"We're off to Edwards Air Force Base in California, Irv. Tell them to crank up *Marine One* and have *Air Force One* turning over now."

Agent Hawkins smiled. "Congratulations, ma'am. We'll have you there before you know it."

SIXTEEN

"*. . . OUR* CNN correspondent, Jane Willoughby, is on the scene at Edwards Air Force Base. Jane?"

"Thank you, Tom. Well, as you've seen, the landing was right out of the textbook, which was not surprising, as Admiral Wiener has a reputation throughout the service as a top-notch pilot.

"The crew of the *Forlorn Hope* is on the stand with Director of Flight Operations Alex Rayne. Yes, and here come our two visitors. As you can see, they are similar to us in many ways, although their skin pigmentation is an almost aqua blue. The man is very large, you can see that he's much taller than Admiral Wiener and Squadron Leader Ryham, both of whom are six-foot-four. The woman is, according to sources here, the man's mother, and—oh, Tom, here comes President Catesby. She's walking up the steps, shaking hands with Colonels Monroe, Conger-Levin, and Fournier. Now she's greeting Commander Rodgers, Major Caldwell, and Squadron Leader Ryham. The president is now welcoming the two extraterrestrials, both of whom seem to speak English . . . they're sharing a laugh about something . . . the man is now motioning to the president to greet Admiral Wiener . . . I don't know why he would do that . . .

"Now the president is shaking hands with Admiral Wiener. They're still shaking hands . . . still shaking hands . . . still shaking hands . . . I think I saw a tear out of the president's eye . . . she must be relieved to see the crew safely arrived home on this historic occasion . . . still shaking hands . . .

"The admiral has kissed the president's cheek . . . I wonder if she minds his taking such a liberty . . . oh! Now the president is kissing the admiral's cheek . . . now they've both kissed on the lips!

"Uh . . . Tom, they're still kissing . . . now they're embracing . . . looks like a very *tight* embrace . . . now they're *really* kissing . . . now they've stopped. . . . they're looking into each other's eyes . . . the admiral has said something and the president has nodded her head and has tears from both eyes now . . . they're kissing again . . . still kissing . . . still kissing . . . still kissing . . ."

Penguin Putnam Inc.
Online

Your Internet gateway to a virtual environment with
hundreds of entertaining and enlightening books
from Penguin Putnam Inc.

*While you're there, get the latest buzz on
the best authors and books around—*

Tom Clancy, Patricia Cornwell, W.E.B. Griffin,
Nora Roberts, William Gibson, Robin Cook,
Brian Jacques, Catherine Coulter, Stephen King,
Ken Follett, Terry McMillan, and many more!

**Penguin Putnam Online is located at
http://www.penguinputnam.com**

PENGUIN PUTNAM NEWS

Every month you'll get an inside look at our upcom-
ing books and new features on our site. This is an
ongoing effort to provide you with the most
up-to-date information about
our books and authors.

Subscribe to Penguin Putnam News at
http://www.penguinputnam.com/newsletters

TWO-TIME HUGO AWARD-WINNING AUTHOR

ALLEN STEELE

❑ **CLARKE COUNTY, SPACE**   **0-441-11044-4/$5.99**

❑ **ALL-AMERICAN ALIEN BOY**   **0-441-00460-1/$5.99**

❑ **THE JERICHO ITERATION**   **0-441-00271-4/$5.99**

❑ **LABYRINTH OF NIGHT**   **0-441-46741-5/$6.50**

❑ **OCEANSPACE**   **0-441-00685-X/$21.95**

❑ **ORBITAL DECAY**   **0-441-49851-5/$5.99**

❑ **THE TRANQUILLITY ALTERNATIVE**
                                                              0-441-00433-4/$5.99

Prices slightly higher in Canada

Payable by Visa, MC or AMEX only ($10.00 min.), No cash, checks or COD. Shipping & handling:
US/Can. $2.75 for one book, $1.00 for each add'l book; Int'l $5.00 for one book, $1.00 for each
add'l. Call (800) 788-6262 or (201) 933-9292, fax (201) 896-8569 or mail your orders to:

Penguin Putnam Inc.   Bill my: ❑ Visa ❑ MasterCard ❑ Amex _____(expires)
P.O. Box 12289, Dept. B   Card# _____
Newark, NJ 07101-5289   Signature _____
Please allow 4-6 weeks for delivery.
Foreign and Canadian delivery 6-8 weeks.

Bill to:
Name _____
Address _____City _____
State/ZIP _____Daytime Phone # _____
Ship to:
Name _____Book Total $ _____
Address _____Applicable Sales Tax $ _____
City _____Postage & Handling $ _____
State/ZIP _____Total Amount Due $ _____
This offer subject to change without notice.   Ad # N212 (2/01)

JOSHUA DANN

wants to know
Do You Believe in Yesterday?

Timeshare Unlimited isn't just your typical travel agency. It's a time-travel agency...and its clients can voyage to the past. Of course, sometimes they don't want to return—not surprising when you consider the sense of excitement, hope, and endless possibilities that await them in the land of yesteryear.

As head of security for Timeshare Unlimited, ex-LAPD cop John Surrey, past, present, and future will never be the same...

"Clever...well-crafted...highly enjoyable."—_Starlog_
TIMESHARE   __0-441-00457-1/$5.99

TIMESHARE: SECOND TIME AROUND
                                 __0-441-00567-5/$5.99

Prices slightly higher in Canada

Payable by Visa, MC or AMEX only ($10.00 min.), No cash, checks or COD. Shipping & handling: US/Can. $2.75 for one book, $1.00 for each add'l book; Int'l $5.00 for one book, $1.00 for each add'l. Call (800) 788-6262 or (201) 933-9292, fax (201) 896-8569 or mail your orders to:

Penguin Putnam Inc.
P.O. Box 12289, Dept. B
Newark, NJ 07101-5289
Please allow 4-6 weeks for delivery.
Foreign and Canadian delivery 6-8 weeks.

Bill my: ❏ Visa ❏ MasterCard ❏ Amex _____ (expires)
Card# _____
Signature _____

Bill to:
Name _____
Address _____ City _____
State/ZIP _____ Daytime Phone # _____
Ship to:
Name _____ Book Total $ _____
Address _____ Applicable Sales Tax $ _____
City _____ Postage & Handling $ _____
State/ZIP _____ Total Amount Due $ _____
This offer subject to change without notice.